Axis Stone Mysteries

THE
HORSE ARM CASE

G. L. Keady

Published in Australia in 2023
by Big Island Publishing

Big Island Publishing
PO Box 3027, Tuross Head, 2537, NSW, Australia.
www.bigislandpublishing.au

ISBN:
Print: 978-0-6459738-9-1
Digital: 978-0-6459739-0-7

Edited by: Canon Doyle
Cover design and art: Brandon Evans-Keady

TABLE OF CONTENTS

CHAPTER
ONE

JUTTING out into Hudson Bay, Pier 25 resembles a massive concrete finger. This pier is due for development, slated to ultimately become the second-largest park in Manhattan after Central Park. However, for now, in 1988, it appears as bare as when it was first constructed in 1935.

At a ripe old age of seventy-five, J. Wellington Smythe has faithfully fished the end of Pier 25 at sunset since his boyhood. He rarely catches much. Yet, on one rare occasion while fishing with worms, he hooked and landed a twenty-kilo Atlantic Sturgeon. But most often, if he manages to catch anything at all, it's likely to be a whitefish or a pike.

Today, however, was different. His fishing rod creaked and protested under the strain, perspiration dripped from his chin; he had hooked something really big. The catch wasn't fighting much, rather like a dead weight. Regardless, it reminded him of twenty years ago when he hooked the huge sturgeon. Rumours of his battle spread, a crowd gathered, cheering him on in the hope he could land a massive fish. A friend of Smythe's arrived with a gaff, waiting patiently to assist with hoisting the catch twenty feet from the water to the wharf.

The struggle lasted an hour. Smythe was exhausted but knew he was close to bringing it to the surface. With a swirl and a collective gasp from the crowd, they all saw what Smythe had caught break the surface of Hudson Bay in the fading light of the day. But it wasn't a sturgeon, nor even a fish—it was the torso of a dead horse.

~ ~ ~

When Smythe, his friend with the gaff, and several others finally managed to get the gruesome corpse onto the wharf, the crowd formed a circle around it to gawk. Word had spread far enough to alert a news crew who had been covering a car accident in nearby Tribeca.

As dusk fell, the news crew—consisting of a reporter, camera operator, sound technician, and lighting professional—set up to cover the strange event for the late news. That's when Smythe noticed something odd about the headless horse; its stomach was stitched up with thread. While the news team filmed, Smythe knelt down beside his catch and used a filleting knife to open the stitches. What happened next caused onlookers to vomit, recoil in shock, and express horror. From the horse's gut slipped a severed human arm.

~ ~ ~

After the opal case that had taken me to Hollywood, Vegas, and Frisco, I decided to expand my horizons. Now that I was flush, I relocated to New York. I chose the Big Apple because it was where I'd been raised as a kid and where my parents had successfully earned a living writing hard-boiled detective crime fiction pulps—the sort everyone read during the '60s, '70s, and '80s while commuting to work. Their racy yarns brought them some infamy and wealth, some of which became an inheritance that still provides me an annual income today.

My parents had rented a small studio in the Regis Offices in Hell's Kitchen, Lower Manhattan. Kept mothballed for me, the office provided the ideal location to base Axis Stone Investigations, USA. My ultimate plan was to franchise ASI nation-wide and internationally. I'd mothballed the Sydney office for the time being, expecting it to eventually become the headquarters for ASI Asia, Pacific.

I'd only been in town a few days and realised I'd need to hire a PA to spread my wings, so I advertised for one for free on Hell's Kitchen Radio. Accustomed to the smaller size of Sydney, I wasn't prepared for the flood of applicants. Over the phone, I managed to narrow them down and scheduled personal interviews at the office. I had specific taste preferences that could only be sated with a personal meeting.

I was down to the last two applicants after an arduous task. The candidates had been waiting in the corridor outside while I conducted five-minute interviews in the two-room office, one-on-one.

The penultimate applicant had a lovely pair of shapely, bare legs. She sat on the couch with them crossed, one leg riding up and down on the other. I asked her the standard set of questions I'd asked all the others. She didn't cut it.

I had high hopes for the final applicant. With her shapely legs in skin-tight black hollow-out pants, crossed with one leg riding on the other, high heel sandals—she wouldn't let me get a word in—pass. I'd been through so many applicants and none of them made the cut. I wondered whether it was me and my peculiar taste, or to my greenness of East Coast manner. A faint knock at the door snapped me out of my reverie. It seemed I'd miscalculated; there was one more applicant.

I called out, "Come in."

She glided into the office with all the rhythm of a 1970s soul singer, sat on the couch without crossing her lovely bare brown legs that extended from her navy skirt. I noticed her sandaled feet adorned with red toenail polish and a seriously intelligent look in her big brown eyes—physically, she was ticking all the boxes.

She handed me her curriculum vitae. I looked it over.

"Miss Lee... a post-grad master's in journalism... a thirty-two-year-old single mom..."

She beamed a big smile, "That's me, warts 'n all."

I looked up at her from the CV, "Answer me this, you mention here that you're into prog-rock music, why?"

She scrunched up her nose cutely, "Um, it doesn't have an expiration date."

I nodded approvingly. "Hours are weird, money's average but your boss is to die for."

"So when do I get to meet him then?" she teased.

I stood and offered my hand. "That's the answer I've been after. You're hired. Start tomorrow at nine A.M."

And so it came to pass that after interviewing forty-four applicants, I'd settled on Miss Kendy Lee.

~ ~ ~

We descended in the rickety old elevator together, heading down to the lobby. Upon our arrival, Linus, the elderly manager of the residences, emerged from his ground-floor apartment. In his mid-seventies, his once jet-black Afro hairstyle, as I remembered it, had now been trimmed short and was salt-and-pepper. But age hadn't diminished his cheerful disposition.

He greeted us with a warm smile. "Well, hello, AS. Is this the lass you were looking for? Hell, you had more visitors today than a Broadway audition."

I'm sure he assumed it was a novel way for me to meet women.

"Linus Regis, meet my new PA, Miss Kendy Lee," I introduced.

The perfect gentleman, Linus removed his cap and gently shook Kendy's hand. "I've known Junior here since he was a mere sprog. He's a good stick."

I could see by the expression on Kendy's face that she needed to translate the word 'stick' into 21st-century speak.

"Linus owns the building," I explained. "He originally rented the office that's now mine to my folks."

"Oh, were they PIs?"

"No, a crime fiction writing team."

"Nice to meet you, Linus. Thank you, Mr Stone. See you in the

A.M."

Linus and I watched her walk toward the front door with all the grace of a gazelle.

"Ooo wee, you can sure pick 'em," Linus remarked.

"Linus, I need to ask you something about Mum and Dad."

"Sure thing, son, walk this way."

"I'm not old enough," I quipped as he led me, chuckling at my sense of humour, into his apartment.

The décor was a monument to the 20th Century. I was expecting at any moment Lionel Richie to burst out of the kitchen singing 'Hello, is it me you're looking for?'

"Siddown, boy, what's on your mind?" Linus asked.

I settled into a well-worn, moth-eaten armchair. It was as comfy as hell; they sure don't make them like that anymore. There was a pungent aroma of coffee.

"Yep, coffee, just brewed. How'd you take it?" he said, hobbling off to the kitchen. "Keep talking; I can hear you. I'm not completely deaf."

"Just black will be fine," I called back. I peered at the bookrack adorning the side wall. In prime position was a collection of at least a hundred of Carter Stone paperbacks. "You must have the best collection of Dad's books?"

Linus returned, handed me a mug of coffee, sat in his favourite armchair, put on a pair of oval John Lennon reading glasses, and glanced at the collection of novels. "Yep, sure do, every one of them."

I took a sip of coffee; it was excellent. "A couple of cases ago I was hired by Winston Lovejoy. His daughter had been kidnapped in the Philippines."

Linus stripped off his glasses, chewing on the left temple tip with an astounded look on his craggy old face. "That's a name familiar to me." His expression reminded me of Morgan Freeman in the film 'A Good Person.'

"Lovejoy said he knew the folks personally. When I wrapped the case, he sent me a text to talk to a guy named Jeremy Yates at the

New York Hermetic Order of the Golden Dawn. Do you know anything about that?"

Linus nodded slowly, thoughtfully. "Seems the time has come, boy, for you to know the truth. Now, hear me out; there's some to tell, and you ain't gonna like it. You see, your folks didn't die of heart failure, son; they was murdered."

It was as though I'd been slapped in the face with a wet fish. "Whoa! That's one hell of an insinuation, Linus. Can you prove it?"

"Well, in order to do that, you'll need to hear out my cousin Booker in Brooklyn Heights."

CHAPTER
TWO

We hailed a taxi in front of the Regis Offices and climbed into the back. Linus gave the driver directions, and the yellow vehicle merged into the line of traffic.

"In 1988, the year your folks died, there was a news report about a recreational fisherman catching something unusual from Pier 25."

"Weird?" I echoed.

"Well, it wasn't a fish. It was the body of a horse."

"A horse? I'll be damned."

"But that's only half it. The horse's gut broke open, and out spewed a severed human arm."

"You're kidding me."

"No, son, I kid you not. So, as you would expect, when your mum and dad heard about this event, they figured it'd make a fine plot for a book, so they went to investigate. You do know that your mum, Denise, was one hell of a writer herself, but back then, she was never going to get a break being female. Any rate, let me tell you, she was the brains behind the writing team."

"Really? I never knew that. I just assumed she did the research."

I could see out the window that the driver had taken Centre Street, heading for the Brooklyn Bridge. I wondered to myself why 'Centre' was spelled the English way and not 'Center' in American.

"Booker knows heaps more than me," Linus continued, "but when the cops dropped the horse arm case, well, that was like a red flag to the Stones; they knew something was off, so they went to see Booker."

"Why your cousin?"

"Well, since day one after I introduced them, your folks struck up a close friendship with Booker. See, from 1965 right up till 1988, Booker worked for the County Coroner's Office as an assistant mortician. Man, he gave your folks so many leads for their books."

I got it. Booker did autopsies, probably dealt with John Does. I could see how invaluable he'd be for them.

"So how did he help with the horse arm case?"

"I'll let Booker tell you that, but that arm ended up at the City Morgue while Booker was on duty."

The taxi pulled up outside a Brooklyn Brownstone. I paid the driver, and then Linus led me to the front door. A coded knock, and the door opened to a tall Afro-American in his mid-seventies with a good physique for his age. Bald, with a warm, friendly demeanour, he stared long and hard at me as if matching my face with a distant memory.

Then he cracked a smile and said, "I know who this young feller is; no-one else could bear such a striking resemblance to both his wonderful parents. You're Axis Stone. Goddamn, I used to give you lollipops. Come in, son."

He led the way along a dimly lit corridor.

"Now I remember you. I didn't know you as Booker; to me, you were always just Unk," I said.

Booker chuckled as he took us into the living room.

"I took a chance on you being home Book," Linus said.

We all took seats.

"Ain't going nowhere these days, Linus; mostly I binge-watch TV shows on the idiot box."

"I brought Junior here because, now he's a PI and old enough, it's time he learnt the truth."

With watery old eyes, Booker studied my face, then he nodded gracefully in agreement with his cousin. He told me about his working relationship with my mum and dad and how so many victims in their novels were based on his actual cases. Thirty years at the New York City Morgue had imparted him with a veritable profusion of stories. One story led to another, so eventually, I needed to delicately interrupt him.

"Tell me, Unk, why do you suspect foul play with the death of my folks?" That certainly put the brakes on his reminiscing.

"Well, when your daddy was brought in, I took it upon myself to check the pathology. The BNP test for heart disease showed negative, which contradicted the Coroner's report. When your mother Denise expressed her concerns to me, I took it upon myself to do more pathology and turned up the presence of a nerve agent that would have given the appearance of a coronary."

"Did you report that to the Coroner?"

"No, son, I didn't. At the time, with the particular Chief Medical Officer, colour was of concern to him."

Linus could tell Booker was getting upset and opted to give him some encouragement. "Go on, Book, tell him."

Booker took a deep breath, then continued. "A while later, I found myself in the same predicament with your sweet mother." He choked up and bowed his head, pinching the bridge of his nose between his fingers. "I found the same fraud, son," he looked back up at me, and I could feel his pain. "I'm sorry, son, there was nothing I could do."

Linus got up and put a consoling hand on Booker's shoulder. "Book handed in his resignation after his findings were rejected twice by the same racist Coroner."

All the emotion with the revelation had me up pacing the carpet, my mind racing. I stopped with a thought. "And you believe their murders are related to this horse arm case?"

Booker looked me in the eye and said forcefully, "Absolutely, I do."

"But why?" I asked.

"It was the first time they were investigating a true crime," Booker said, calmer. "Every other time they were just making stuff up off'r-a fact."

"Hmm, what else do you remember that might help?" I asked.

He thought a moment, then said, "Yeah, there was something about the Golden Dawn Society."

That hit a nerve. Obviously, the next step would be to follow up on Jeremy Yates. Made me wonder if my folks were members.

Linus added, "I think Denise finished the book."

He had my attention. "A true-crime book?"

"Yeah, but don't know that it was ever published," Linus claimed.

That gave me an idea. "So, somewhere there must be a manuscript that could well hold clues to what might have got them both murdered."

Booker and Linus exchanged a smile, recognising the same curiosity in me that had driven my folks as researchers.

CHAPTER
THREE

I was at my desk, engrossed in a phone call when Kendy entered the office carrying a small cardboard box. With her hair up, leather jacket, black, short, leather skirt, and an official 1975 U.S Tour Zeppelin T-shirt, she certainly embodied the ASI ethos. She opened the box, handed me a coffee, and a croissant as I finished the call.

"Hey, Kendy, is it possible to hire two PAs for the same job simultaneously?"

She grinned, "Yes, but it would cost you double."

We both dunked our croissants.

"Right," I said, "We're officially on a case."

"Hey that's exciting. Like, what is it?"

"I have reason to believe my parents were murdered back in 1988. The Coroner's report stated they both died from heart failure, no suspicious circumstances. However, last night, I learned from a reliable source, a former mortuary attendant at the New York City Morgue at the time, that he discovered they'd both been poisoned by the same nerve agent."

Kendy stopped eating and stared at me incredulously. "Like, you're kidding me, right?"

"No, Kendy, I'm not."

"So, did he report it?"

"No, he's a person of colour, so in 1988, he had no say. Racism to the max; his findings were ignored, and he quit his job. So, your job today is to go to the NYPD archives and search everything they have on a 1988 Horse Arm Case, then do the same at the New York Post."

Kendy looked at me as if I had just stolen her lunch money. "Horse arm? Like, horses don't have arms, right?"

"This one did. In 1988, it was snagged by a guy fishing in the Hudson, and when he got it onto Pier 25, it burst open, and a human arm spewed out of it."

"Ew, you've put me right off my croissant. Like, how gross."

"Yes, kind of unsavoury, but I want to know all about it. While you're doing that, I'll be interviewing someone downtown at the Hermetic Order of the Golden Dawn."

She gave me that incredulous stare again. "The Hermetic Order of the Golden Dawn? Serious? Like who are you? Harry Potter?"

I shot her my favourite private detective look and told her sternly, "You'll get used to it."

~ ~ ~

I stepped out of the taxi on 53rd Street, just outside the offices of the Golden Dawn Society. The day was sweltering with humidity. I glanced upward between the towering buildings, eyeing a patch of sky. There was a hint of rain in the air.

Entering through the Golden Dawn bookshop was necessary— the place had seen better days. As I stepped inside the shop void of customers, a striking young woman with glasses and her hair elegantly pinned up noticed me. She was dressed in a navy jacket and skirt. The shop exuded an ancient scent, reminiscent of a library. There wasn't a single space in the entire room that wasn't occupied by books.

"Hello there, are you a member?" she inquired smoothly.

I surmised that she must spend most of her time fending off book-mites with a feather duster.

"No, but perhaps my parents were. I'd be happy to join if you're the member paradigm," I replied, trying to inject a touch of humour.

If you looked up 'horny librarian' in the dictionary, her photograph would undoubtedly be there.

She raised a sceptical eyebrow over her horn-rimmed glasses and purred, "Surely you can do better than that, sir?"

"I thought it was original enough. I have an appointment with Jeremy Yates."

"Ah, yes, you must be Mr Stone. Follow me; he's expecting you."

"That would be my pleasure."

I enjoyed following her down the narrow corridor, discreetly observing the sway of her posterior and her long, shapely legs. She stopped at a wood-panelled door, opened it, and ushered me inside. I turned to offer her another witty line, but she had vanished. A male voice redirected my attention.

"Mr Stone, son of Carter and Denise... well, I never."

He exuded debonair charm, with a receding hairline and a dapper navy-blue suit. He walked toward me, extending his hand for a handshake, which I accepted.

"Mr Yates, thank you for seeing me. It's a pleasure to meet you."

"Jeremy to you. Aren't you just the spitting image of your dad with your mother's eyes. This way."

In his late sixties, his speech bore the hallmarks of a Harvard-educated pedigree.

While following him, I inquired, "Who was that lovely lady who greeted me?"

"My daughter Lisa. Yes, she's quite special. Axis, do you mind if I call you by your Christian name?"

"Be my guest—"

He led me into a spacious office that resembled more of a small mausoleum, akin to my vision of a 19th Century Gentleman's Club. It reeked of occultism. I glanced up at a large framed photograph of Aleister Crowley, staring down at me from the wall. It was eerie; it felt like his eyes were tracking my every move.

Yates motioned me to sit on the old Chesterfield lounge. He took a seat opposite me in a matching armchair and crossed his legs. I could tell from the soles of his brown lace-up shoes that they were new.

"So, you worked with Sir Winston?"

"I'm a PI and had the privilege of being in his employ for a case a while back."

"Yes, the kidnapping of his daughter, if I'm not mistaken, happily resolved as well."

"News travels fast."

"Especially when it's family… and we consider you family, Axis, just as it was for your father and mother."

A quick scan of the room revealed nothing more to add to my initial assessment, except for a framed black and white portrait photograph of Madame Helena Blavatsky, the Russian mystic who founded the Theosophical Society in the late 19th Century. She, too, had piercing eyes. Both portraits were a bit unsettling for the uninitiated.

"Never had them pegged as members of a secret society though."

"Oh, we're not so much a secret order, more a group of like-minded researchers of hermetic theosophy."

"Aha, so, you personally knew my parents?"

"Friends, though they were much closer to my predecessor, Colonel Witten."

"Maybe you can help me. My parents wrote their last book in 1988. It was never published. It was a departure from their regular crime fiction, a non-fiction work, true crime. But the manuscript is missing, and Linus…"

"Linus Regis?"

"Yes, he believes it could well have been on a 4.5-inch diskette that my mum might have hidden, and this place seems a likely spot."

Yates paused, deep in thought, and then said, "Here? Oh no, I don't think so. However, we can certainly take a look."

He rose and went to an old metal filing cabinet, pulled open the top drawer and rifled through files, muttering to himself all the while.

"Hmm, let's see… Radcliffe… Robertson… Sebastian, ah, here we are… Stone."

He returned to his chair with a thick folder, sat down, and opened it.

"There's something on the cover," I observed.

He closed it and examined the cover, looking quite surprised. "So there is… it says, 'I'll tell you where to look but not what to see.' Hmm, that's a little cryptic, don't you think?" He opened the folder. "There's quite a bit to go through. Here, take it with you to study," he said, handing it over.

"There's no disk?"

"Doesn't seem to be, but among the documents, there could well be a clue to its location. Especially with that cryptic note on the outside in your mother's handwriting."

I looked at the message again. "You're certain it's her writing?"

"Yes, I'd have to say so. Your father wrote like a doctor, illegible, but your mother's writing was neat and graceful, like her."

Yates stood, signalling the end of our meeting. I tucked the folder under my arm and followed him back the way we came. We stopped before the bookshop.

"Thanks, Jeremy. It seems that every time I solve one problem, it leads to another mystery."

"Comes with the name, my boy. Keep in touch."

We shook hands, and as I passed through the shop, Lisa caught up with me. I halted.

"Did you find what you were looking for?"

I gave her the once-over and injected a bit of innuendo into my response.

"That depends."

She pursed her scarlet lips. "On what, exactly?"

"On what I need at the moment and what's on offer."

She shot me a sly smile. "Let's just say there's plenty on offer. So, what are you in need of?"

"Your number and a promise."

She placed her Apple watch next to my pocket, and my phone

chimed with an alert.

"That's the number. What's the promise?"

"That's yet to be revealed."

I headed for the exit, aware of Lisa's gaze on me, and heard her mutter to herself loud enough for me to hear.

"Oh, I'm sure you be pleased with what's revealed."

CHAPTER
FOUR

I was punching data into my desktop computer when Kendy breezed into the office. She flopped despondently in the chair opposite me.

"My first mission was like a total failure. Not a thing in police records, and weirdest thing of all, nothing in newspaper archives… it's like it never happened."

"I've been surfing online, same, nothing. That can only mean one thing: The Firm got hold of it and buried it."

"The Firm, what, like the FBI? Why?"

"It must be implicated in something to do with national security. Wait."

"What?"

"Linus said it was in a news report, there might be footage. Here, go through this, see if you can find anything," I said, handing her the folder. "We're looking for a computer disk."

Kendy took the folder to her office annexed to mine. She looked up at the wood-panelled wall overlaid with framed front covers of Carter Stone Mysteries. The opposite wall was exposed bricks and it was plastered with photographs of Carter and Denise. She put the folder on her desk and wandered over to the wall of photos. One particular photo attracted her; it was Carter with the members of the British rock band Pink Floyd, autographed and titled 'Madison Square Garden, A Momentary Lapse of Reason Tour 1987.' She returned to the desk, sat, and opened the folder. After thumbing through it, she found something out of place: the cover art of Pink Floyd's, Another Brick in the Wall.

She sat back and mumbled to herself. "What the heck is this, like, so random?"

Curious, she got up and went back to the wall of photos. She removed the photo of Carter backstage with Pink Floyd from the wall and checked the back of it.

She called out, "AS, got a minute? You need to like check this out."

I came in to see what she had.

"Something in the folder?"

"Kind of... it's to do with this picture from the wall," she said, handing the photograph over.

"Yeah, the folks were Floyd fanatics."

"But this was in the folder."

She showed me the 'Another Brick in the Wall' art.

"Huh? Why would that be in the folder?"

"That's what I thought, but look—" She said, touching a loose brick in the facade and then tried to free it. "It's like loose or something."

I took over and prised the brick out. In the space behind it was a 4.5-inch diskette. I held it up triumphantly.

"Well done, kiddo, sheer genius!"

"Now all we need to do is like find out how to retrieve the data from it. I've got a computer nerd friend?"

"Cool, get onto that. I've got a lead on the CBS news reporter who covered the horse arm story in '88."

We got onto our respective cellphones.

~ ~ ~

Kendy was leaving her friend Dwip's apartment. Dwip, Asian, short-cropped hair, thin, sexy, wearing short shorts, bare feet and a loose singlet, no bra, gave Kendy a hug, and then they kissed passionately. Both of them heavy breathing with arousal, Kendy pulled away.

"I've gotta go—"

Dwip smiled lovingly. "Bye sexy baby... I'll try and get it done tonight, okay?"

Kendy held open her palm presenting a flash-drive. "Stick it on here."

Dwip grabbed her hand, pulled her close and snatched the drive. "Hmm, stick it in you," she purred sexily and then poked out her tongue.

"Next time beautiful," Kendy said before blowing her a kiss.

~ ~ ~

I got out of the taxi and made my way to the intercom of the Perry Street apartments in Greenwich Village. I located the name I sought: L. Parks, Apartment 1A. Luck was on my side as an elderly lady with a walking stick struggled with the entrance door. I assisted her and then slipped inside, successfully bypassing the security.

I knocked on the door of the ground-floor apartment. After a while, the door opened as far as the night chain would allow, revealing an eye peering at me through the gap.

"Oh, yes, come in," she said and unhitched the chain.

She was elderly and confined to a wheelchair. "It's in the living room. I don't know what's wrong with it... must be the satellite dish."

"Are you Liz Parks, ma'am?" I inquired.

She glared at me as if I were being particularly dense and snapped, "Of course I am. You should know that."

"I'm not the cable guy, ma'am. My name is Axis Stone, I'm a private detective."

Her face froze, and she glared at me with the sort of contempt one usually reserves for a particularly obnoxious pest.

"Axis Stone?" she all but yelled. "What do you mean by forcing your way in here under false pretences?"

"Please, calm down, Miss Parks... I only want to talk to you. It'll will take—"

But she would have none of it. "Shoo! Out! Go on before I call the cops!"

She rammed her wheelchair into my shins and jammed me against the door.

"I just want to ask you about the horse arm case. Ouch!"

"Never heard of it. Get out!"

She had me pinned against the door.

"Please, it got both my parents killed."

"I know who you are… you even look like him!"

"You talking about my father?"

"Damn right I am, now out!"

How's that? I mean—"

"Not for you to know… now get out!"

I managed to squeeze out from being pressed against the door and pleaded with her. "Look, you were a CBS crime reporter… you know more than anyone how tough it is to investigate a murder."

"Yes, I know," she said irritably, "don't badger me!"

"I just need a few answers, please!"

"Can't help. Out!"

I dropped my business card in her lap. "If you change your mind." I let myself out.

~ ~ ~

It was dusk when Kendy approached the door to let herself into Axis Stone Investigations. As she inserted the key, the door opened. She entered.

"AS, are you there?" She asked tentatively. It was then she recognised that the place had been turned over. Shocked, she backed out of the door and hurried downstairs. Thinking to alert Linus, she knocked on his door—it swung open. It was a repeat of what she'd already experienced—she crept inside.

Only a standard lamp was on in the living room, casting eerie shadows in the dim lighting. Then she saw Linus sprawled out on the floor, and it took her breath away. She knelt down and felt for a pulse. It was faint. She pulled out her phone and speed-dialled me.

I got out of the taxi and rushed inside the Regis building. Kendy met me at the door to Linus' apartment. She led me inside. By then, Linus was conscious and sitting in his armchair.

"Mate, are you all right? What happened?" I inquired.

"I'm fine, I'm fine, some bastard barged in here and whacked me from behind."

"Office is a mess… the perp was obviously looking for something."

"Could only be the disk," I snarled.

I sat on the couch to think. Kendy sat on the arm of Linus' chair and held the old man's thin hand. Linus was enjoying the attention.

"Who the hell knew the disk might be here? Us, Booker, Yates, Winston maybe? That's about it."

"You don't think Booker might've contacted the Coroner's office?" Linus figured.

"Why would he do that?" I questioned.

"Maybe to get you a lead. You heard him; he ain't got much to do with himself nowadays."

I got a text alert. It said, 'FBI agent Jake Rixon interviewed me in '88 about horse arm. Come at 10 tonight; I'll fill you in. Liz.'

Kendy asked, "News?"

"A lead and maybe more. Want me to call the cops, Linus?"

With a wave of his hand, he declared, "No, no, that ain't necessary unless you wanna report your office being turned over."

"Nah, listen up then, whoever's after the disk is desperate; we'll need to be more vigilant."

We exchanged a silent but anxious stare. I got up and made a call while pacing the floor.

"Hello, can you put me through to agent Jake Rixon? I'll wait… Oh, okay, can I leave him a message? You have my number, ask him to call me about a case… I'm in New York… Stone… Axis Stone… Thank you."

"FBI?" Kendy asked.

"Yes. You be alright, Linus? We're going upstairs to clean up."

"No problem. Before that, go to the bureau and open the top drawer will you dear," Linus asked Kendy. She did so, took out a pistol and looked at the huge, vintage, Colt .45, amazed, barely able to lift it.

"This old thing?"

Linus chuckled, "Yep, bring it here, girl. The next bastard that comes in here looking for trouble will have to deal with Betsy."

"That thing's a cannon," I said with a laugh.

~ ~ ~

We entered the office, and I stopped just inside the door to survey the clutter. There was stuff everywhere. "What a mess," I muttered under my breath. I got another text alert. It said; 'Meet at the Slaughtered Lamb pub, 4th Street, Greenwich Village at 8 P.M.' It was from Rixon. "Got to meet with FBI agent Rixon at 8 tonight, the Slaughtered Lamb Pub in the Village."

"What sort of pub has a name like that?" Kendy reacted. Just then she got a text alert and told me. "My friend Dwip has transferred the data onto my flash-drive; it's ready for pick-up."

"Can't it be transferred over the net?"

"Not to worry, she lives nearby; I'll pick it up on the way home… do you need it tonight or—?"

"No, no, it's after seven now; you should be getting home. I've got the eight o'clock with Rixon, then Liz Parks at ten. We'll check it in the morning after we clean this mess up."

I straightened the family portrait on the wall on the way out, and we left for the day.

~ ~ ~

Out front, I watched Kendy meld into the throng of peak-hour pedestrians, then crossed the street to head for Canal Street Subway Station. It takes ten minutes from there to the Village.

There was standing room only on the train. It jerked, and a blonde in a mini-skirt with ample curves was forced against me, body to body. We exchanged an awkward but alluring glance. When the train stopped at Greenwich Street Station, she gave me a cute smile and then disappeared with the alighting crowd. I wondered: when you meet someone out of the blue, and you both feel a certain chemistry, but you let it go, did you miss out on an opportunity to meet your soulmate? I quickly dismissed the thought, filing it in the 'you'll never know' basket.

The train stopped at Greenwich Village Station, and I got off.

CHAPTER
FIVE

I walked the narrow, tree-lined Perry Street in Greenwich Village, thinking about how convenient it was that my next appointment with Liz Parks was on the same street. It felt like déjà vu, having already been here earlier today.

The Slaughtered Lamb Pub was on the corner ahead of me. I stopped inside the main bar and scoped the joint. The décor reminded me of Halloween. There were a few patrons scattered about. An old guy at the bar, drinking a pint of ale, stood out like a sore thumb. He was dressed in the mandatory grey suit, white shirt with a thin black necktie. The only thing missing from his '60s get-up was a Fedora. I went over to him, and he kept studying his beer before finally addressing it.

"Stone, I presume, son of the infamous writing team. Hope you're not here researching a pulp; if you are, you're barking up the wrong tree."

I took the barstool next to him and returned the serve. "Does the firm issue a dress code for you guys? Ever think of not standing out in a crowd?"

Rixon leered at me, "There you go, a big mouth like your old man."

He had deep-set eyes and a wrinkled, acne-scarred face, giving him a sinister and untrustworthy countenance.

"I suppose at least you blend with the decor. No, I'm not

researching a novel; I'm a PI investigating two murders."

"What's the accent? You a Brit?"

"No, it's Aussie. Born there, raised here, then back there."

"Okay, I'm listening, for now."

"It's to do with the 1988 Hudson Bay horse arm case."

He took a swig of his beer. "Never happened. It's a myth."

"Well, someone has news footage that belies that."

He slammed his beer down, slammed the stein on the bar, and got up to leave.

"You're wasting my time and yours, sonny," he said irreverently.

"Firstly, I'm not your sonny and secondly, aren't you going to ask how I got your name?"

"Nope, no interest."

"Okay, I'll just go over your head and requisition information through—"

He cut me off, handing me a business card with a snarl, "Here, submit a written request for a criminal record rap sheet on your folks. It costs eighteen bucks. Next time, check FAQ online before wasting a Federal agent's valuable time." After a distasteful side-eye glance, he walked out.

I gestured to the bartender. "A rye over rocks... Got a menu?" He pointed at a menu on the bar. Obviously, he wasn't after a tip with such an abhorrent attitude. "I'll take the inferno burger."

He shot back with a strong New Jersey accent, "It's hot like d' name sez."

"I can handle the heat," I said irritably. I took my drink and moved to a table to distance myself from his bad vibes.

~ ~ ~

With a fire in my belly from the jalapeños, I took to the Perry Street pavement, heading to meet with Liz Parks. After a couple of minutes' walk, I could see a police cordon up ahead, with NYPD vehicles with flashing blue lights. As I got closer, I realised they were outside my destination. When I reached the crime scene barrier tape,

I noticed a detective chatting with a uniformed officer and courteously interrupted.

"Detective? Sir? Can I have a word? I'm a PI."

The rotund detective looked in my direction and acknowledged with a nod. I ducked under the tape and approached him. He looked like the answer to a hostess's prayer at a cannibal barbecue.

He said, "Lieutenant Bixby, you are?"

I flashed my PI ID. "Axis Stone. I'm here to meet Miss Liz Parks at her apartment. What's up?"

"Follow me, Stone."

He led the way inside through a profusion of police officers. Just inside the entrance door, I was provided a pair of overshoes by a female CSI. I slipped them on, then followed Bixby along plastic sheet floor coverings to the Parks apartment. CSI officers were moving in and out through the open apartment door. A few of them moved away for me to see Liz Parks slumped in her wheelchair, dead, with a frozen look of terror on her face.

I started to ask Bixby, "How did—?"

"Look at her left ear," he said gruffly, "a wooden knitting needle has been driven through it into her brain."

I winced, "Jesus."

A female CSI approached Bixby. "Bulldog, it's a wrap here for us, the place has been wiped clean. The perp was a pro."

Bulldog suited him just fine. She wasn't too bad either.

"Now all I need to determine is why some prick would want to murder an old lady in a wheelchair. It wasn't robbery, so let's fact-check… Name was Elizabeth Parks—lived alone, here, correct?"

Bulldog asked, looking at me.

"Um, yeah, as far as I know."

He headed out, and I tailed him. He talked to me even though I was behind him. "What's your interest in her, Stone?"

"She had information on a case I'm working on."

He stopped sharply, and I almost collided with him. "Tell you what, Stone, you're going to sit in my car and satisfy my curiosity…

are you right with that?"

I nodded; he was quite intimidating. "Sure. Not a problem."

We slipped off our overshoes, and I followed him out to his car.

He stopped us at a Ford Explorer. We got in. He was so large he almost took up the entire canopy, with the steering wheel pressed hard against his tummy. He lit a cigarette and, to be polite, held it out the open window, taking a drag and blowing the smoke outside.

"Both my folks died in 1988 months apart. The coroner's report was heart failure in both cases, but a mortuary assistant found traces of a nerve agent in both bodies—the same nerve agent."

"An inquiry?"

"None done. Suspicious."

He took another drag and expelled the smoke out into the night air.

"Go on."

"I only found out about it a couple of days ago. My folks were a well-known crime fiction writing team, but in this instance, they were researching a true crime, which I believe got them murdered."

"How does Parks fit in?"

"She was a CBS crime reporter in 1988 and reported on the murder my folks were researching. I met her earlier today to get her story. She had nothing to say but changed her mind later and texted me to meet her here at ten tonight."

"Hmm, we didn't find a cellphone. Where were you before here?"

"Having a bite at the Slaughtered Lamb Pub up the road."

"Why there?"

"I met someone else connected to the case, though he denies it."

"Who's that?"

"A fed. Liz Parks had texted me his name… he'd interviewed her in 1988 about the case."

"What was this case?"

"The horse arm case," I said, and as I did, it sounded weird to me.

He looked at me like I was out of my mind and questioned with irony, "The horse arm case."

"I know, I know it sounds weird but—"

"Maybe you killed Parks."

"What did I use for a motive? Like I have it in for old ladies in wheelchairs and returned to the scene of the crime to check my work?"

"This is New York, anything is possible," he said, crushing his finished cigarette between his fingers. "I don't know, Stone, but someone out there didn't like Miss Parks. Give me your details."

I handed him a business card. "Will you check on the horse arm case?"

"We'll see," he mumbled, reading my card. "Ah, now I get it, your folks wrote all them pulp crime books? My dad used to read them."

"Carter Stone, a big hit in the '70s and '80s," I said.

"You think this horse arm case got them killed?"

"Sure do."

"You realise this agent might've bumped off Parks?"

"Thought did cross my mind. Look, I'll trade you. Get me the name of the cop in charge of the horse arm case in '88, and I'll give you the name of the Fed."

He swivelled to glare at me with one raised eyebrow. "Don't do deals."

I swung open the door and stepped out. He got in the last word. "Don't leave town, Stone."

I'd heard that before. At least I had another iron in the fire.

~ ~ ~

I walked down the dingy corridor to my Manhattan apartment. When I reached the door and began unlocking it, a figure stepped from the shadows behind me and stuck a gun in my back. I immediately half-raised my hands. He patted me down and took my piece.

"Rixon, you get around."

"Keep your hands up. Inside."

He opened the door and gave me a shove inside.

He ordered, "Lights."

I clapped, and my brand-new sensor lamp in the corner of the living room sprang to life.

"Sit down," he commanded.

I complied and, still with my hands up, sat in an armchair. He sat opposite with the gun on me.

"So, what causes a Fed to turn into a serial killer?"

"Where's the disk?"

"What bloody disk? The horse arm case is a myth, remember?" I said facetiously.

"Cut the smart-arse cracks," he snarled.

"Haven't you heard? I'm the smartest private eye of the year," I quipped. "Can I put my hands down? My fingers are going numb."

"Okay, but don't make any silly moves. You have no idea what you're caught up in, Stone… wasn't it enough it got your folks killed?"

"And tonight you killed again. Why? Didn't she give you what you wanted? Did she know something or too much?"

"Who am I supposed to have killed?"

"Liz Parks. You stabbed her in the ear with a knitting needle."

"A knitting needle? What do you take me for? That's the work of a psycho. She wouldn't have had the disk anyway."

"Then why was she killed? Who else knows about the disk? What's on it that gets people murdered? Why are you sitting there with a gun on me? It was Liz Parks who gave me your name."

"Too many questions. The disk!"

"I don't have the bloody disk."

He was getting riled up. "Alright, alright, here's the deal… get me the disk, and I'll tell you what you need to know." He holstered his gun.

"What's on it that's so important?"

He got up and made for the door, stopped, turned, and growled, "You'll know soon enough."

He dropped my piece on the floor and then slipped out through the door. I quickly collected my piece and made for the window to look down into the street. Rixon came out and got into a waiting car. I figured, if it wasn't the disk, what did Liz Parks know that got her rubbed out? What was she going to tell me about this guy?"

I flopped onto the couch exasperated.

~ ~ ~

The sun beaming in through the living-room window woke me. Just then, like magic, the TV came on. "Thanks Siri," I growled. It was the morning News. I sat up, knuckled my eyes, got up, and walked like a zombie to the bathroom. As I soaped my face, ready for a shave, I heard the Newsreader on TV mention the mysterious murder of an old lady in the Village. I wandered out, shaving cream on my face, and a toothbrush in my mouth, to hear more.

"Former CBS news reporter Liz Parks was found dead in her Greenwich Village apartment last night. Liz was best known for her field reporting."

The vision cut to a young Liz Parks holding a CBS microphone reporting from a crime scene. The on-screen text said, Pier 25, Hudson Bay, 1988.

"I'm at Pier 25, and let me tell you, this is the most bizarre case. A recreational fisherman made a catch he didn't expect in the Hudson River today, the torso of a horse, you heard me, the body of a horse in the Hudson River in the middle of downtown New York, and get this; it had a severed human arm sewn into its belly."

The vision cut from the archive footage back to the News Anchor.

"Liz was fifty-five years old, police are investigating, she will be sadly missed."

I mumbled past my toothbrush, "That was footage of the horse arm..." The Terrible Tango, my ringtone, side-tracked me.

"Siri, turn the TV volume down. Answer the phone. Hello, Stone here."

I continued brushing my teeth.

"You were right about that horse arm case, Stone, it was pulled all right, but I got the name of the investigating officer, he's still a cop but close to retirement."

I pulled out the toothbrush. "Okay Bulldog, a deal's a deal; the Fed in question paid me a hostile visit at my pad last night."

"What do you mean by hostile?"

"Held me at gunpoint."

"Go on… so what'd he want from you?"

"One, for me to shut up and drop the case, and two, a data disk on which my folks kept all their case files."

"Do you have it?"

"No, but I'm on the hunt for it," I lied, not yet sure who to trust.

"Okay, what's the agent's name?"

"Jake Rixon."

"Leave it to me. The cop you wanna talk to is Joe Blake; you can get him at the Albany HQ of New York State Police. You brushing your teeth?"

"Yeah. Now I'm gonna take a shower… you want a running commentary?"

"You gumshoes sure ride the gravy train."

I chuckled as he terminated the call, then I headed back to the bathroom to finish what I'd started.

CHAPTER
SIX

The office was all tidied up and sparkling clean when I arrived. I was totally impressed. Kendy was in her room at her laptop.

"Hey Kendy, good morning... nice job, I couldn't have done better myself."

"Not sure I like subscribe to that," she chuckled.

I enjoyed her sense of humour.

"That aroma is the mug of coffee and the croissant on your desktop," she said.

I grabbed the mug and the croissant and then ambled into her office. She held up a flash-drive.

"Is that what I think?"

"You bet-cher sweet bippy it is."

Croissant in mouth, I pulled up a chair beside her. She popped the drive into her laptop. A folder appeared on her desktop. She clicked it open. There were twelve files.

"So, what do we have?"

"Sequentially numbered chapters for a manuscript by the look of it."

"Excellent. Let's start at the beginning."

I read out loud. "I write this crime novel entitled 'The Last Word' on my own, with a heavy heart. It all began as normal research for our next crime fiction novel, but then it all went wrong.

CS had got a lead from the morning paper..."

"CS?" Kendy asked.

"My dad, Carter Stone, mum always called him CS... So," I continued, "all the news was about the upcoming election, especially now that George Bush had beaten Michael Dukakis to run for the Republican presidential nominee..."

~ ~ ~

1988:

With her ebony hair styled in a bob, a triangular face graced by high cheekbones, radiantly beautiful, Denise Stone glanced up from her 1988 Macintosh SE computer as her husband entered her office, clutching the New York Times spread wide, and a wisp of smoke curling from his cigarette behind it.

"I believe I've uncovered what we've been searching for," he declared in a mid-Atlantic accent.

"The next book?" Denise inquired, her voice tinged with an Aussie accent.

He lowered the newspaper, revealing his striking visage from his towering height of six foot two—handsome and finely featured. Piercing blue eyes gazed forth, complemented by a medium-length dark moustache that accentuated his sharp nose. His jet-black hair was slicked back, and Denise adored her dashing husband, who always maintained a debonair style. This time, he wore a dark blue suit adorned with a subtle pinstripe, a crisp white shirt, and a crimson necktie.

He handed her the tabloid, open to the page he wanted her to read. Denise adjusted the volume of INXS playing on the radio.

"Bizarre," she remarked, lowering the paper, "a guy jags and lands the torso of a horse that contains a human arm."

"Are you thinking a gangland hit or perhaps a cold war spy slaying?" Carter stubbed out his ciggy in the ashtray, placed a loving arm around Denise from behind, pulled her close, and nuzzled her neck.

"All and any of the above."

She snapped him out of his amorous mood. "Right, CS, where do we start?"

He straightened up, looking a little rejected. "Okay, you take the NYPD; I'll get the news footage."

Denise jumped up, turned up 'I Need You Tonight' by INXS on the radio, yelped, "Done," grabbed her coat, and half-dancing to the song, headed out of the office. CS quickly snatched his overcoat from the coat rack and hurried after her.

~ ~ ~

The elevator door to the Detective Bureau at 1st Precinct NYPD opened, and Denise strolled out. The open-plan room was bustling. With the eyes of several officers tracking her, she made her way to a cubicle. She knew the layout; she'd been there before. Smoke was rising from the scruffy form of Joe Blake, sitting with his back to her. He swivelled around and, with a crusty attitude matching his rugged appearance, blew a wad of smoke, greeting her with, "Mrs Stone, Detective Joe Blake."

Denise took a seat. "Thank you for seeing me without notice, Detective. Can you provide any information about last night's case of the severed arm recovered from the horse torso?"

"That's an ongoing investigation. What's your interest, ma'am?" he said with a rich New York accent.

"Research. My husband is an author."

"Anything I'd know?"

"His name is Carter Stone."

A smirk broke on his otherwise sullen face. "Oh sure, the pulp writer who glamorizes private dicks, tits and arse."

"Everyone's a critic," she said tersely.

He crossed his arms defensively, something she didn't miss reading. "So, the case has captured Stone's imagination, huh? Maybe if he writes it, I'll be the detective."

"Maybe, especially if you assist with our research."

He unfurled his arms, picked up an elastic band from the desktop, and began flexing it between his fingers. "Okay, so, white, 30s, prints removed... we're expecting more body parts to turn up now the tide's turned and running in, but that's Maritime, not us. Nothing else distinguishing. Oh, soft hands, not working class. There's always plenty of missing persons in the city, but matching one up with an arm is a tough ask."

"I can understand that. Prints removed? You suspect gang-related, a spy killing, or perhaps a malicious murder?"

"I don't take guesses as a rule, Mrs Stone, but for you, my hunch with prints gone... Mafia."

"Can I get some shots of the arm?"

"Not until the Coroner's office is done with it. Give me a call in a day or so. Here, so you get my name right in the book."

She took his business card and stood. He stubbed his smoke out in the ashtray.

"Thank you, Joe. Can I call you that?"

"Sure can."

"You've been very helpful."

~ ~ ~

CS was on the chaotic news floor of CBS Broadcast Center.

"Seriously, this is like pulling teeth," CS complained.

"Read my lips, Mr Stone, I don't have the authority to give you a copy. Look, I've hit a brick wall in every direction I've tried to go with this," a young Liz Parks complained to Carter, sitting opposite her. They were both frustrated. Carter tapped a filterless cigarette on his thumbnail, then lit it with a gold Dunhill lighter.

"You're the third person to hit me up for a copy in the last hour," she whined.

"Oh really? Who were the others?"

"First was a Fed, got his card here somewhere," she mumbled, searching for it under the clutter of her desktop. Couldn't find it. "Next was a real jerk... only a few minutes ago, you just missed him...

like he wouldn't take no for an answer. I gave him the bum's rush...
no idea who he was. Looked Middle Eastern."

"Could you at least try to get me a copy, Liz?" He lowered his
voice conspiratorially. "I'll happily compensate you for the trouble."
That got her attention; he'd found the ticket. "Perhaps a hundred
bucks?"

She leaned forward, side-eyeing the rest of the room. "One and
a half, cash."

"Done," CS snapped, relieved.

He followed her lead, and she walked him to the elevators.

"Meet me on 57th Street, across from the entrance in fifteen
minutes. I'll have the tape."

~ ~ ~

57th Street was bustling with heavy traffic. CS, cigarette in hand,
waited anxiously across from the entrance of the CBS Broadcast
Center, checking his wristwatch. More than fifteen minutes had
elapsed, and he began to suspect that he was being stood up. Then,
he spotted Liz emerging from the building. He promptly discarded
his cigarette, crushing it underfoot, and prepared the cash to pay for
the tape.

Liz cautiously navigated the spaces between parked cars and
stepped onto the bustling street. CS watched with growing
trepidation as a motorbike accelerated toward Liz. She froze in
response to the approaching danger, and though CS shouted a
warning, his voice was drowned out by the deafening roar of the
bike's engine.

The motorcycle collided with Liz, sending her hurtling into the
air. She landed with a brutal impact on the road, her motionless body
sprawled out. The bike quickly sped away, leaving a scene of shock
and chaos in its wake.

CS immediately rushed onto the street and positioned himself
protectively over Liz, guiding passing traffic around her to prevent
further harm. Onlookers on the pavement were visibly shaken by the

harrowing incident. Spotting an elderly couple nearby, the man capturing tourist photos, CS urgently instructed them to call for an ambulance.

Amid the commotion, CS noticed the VHS tape lying on the ground. It was crushed and mangled, with the tape hanging out in tatters, rendering it utterly useless. Yet, amidst this wreckage, it was the sight of Liz's contorted form that weighed most heavily on his heart.

~ ~ ~

CS was pacing the office floor while Denise was making coffee. She stopped him pacing with a mug. He pulled two cigarettes out of a pack and lit them both with his lighter, handing one to Denise.

"So, we have two suspects."

"You're assuming it wasn't an accident."

He propped on the edge of his desk. "Her neck is broken; she'll never walk again. That biker saw her, could've avoided her... he knew what he was doing. He hit her without coming off himself; that was sharp stunt work."

"I agree we treat it as intentional."

The phone rang, and Denise answered it. "Hello. Yes, oh you did? Regis Building, 66 St. James Street, Lower Manhattan, top floor. Oh, that's nearby. Yes, you can walk here from there. See you soon." She hung up. "Well, this'll be interesting. Tourists from Kentucky witnessed the accident and took photos. They just picked up the prints from Photocrosmat. They'll be here in five minutes."

"How'd they find us?"

"They recognised you, then found us in the phonebook."

It wasn't long after a quick tidy up there was a knock at the door. Denise stubbed out her cigarette and answered the door. She opened it to two country types in their fifties. With a pocketbook under her arm, thin and tall in stature, she was wearing a floral dress and a pillbox hat that went out in the fifties. He was in a wrinkled brown suit that had had its day and holding a brown Fedora in his hand.

"Hi there, I'm Denise Stone, and you're...?"

She answered in a nervous, small voice, "We're the Wilsons, Reg and Mertle."

"Pleased to meet you both. Come in. I'd like you to meet Carter Stone."

They were both in awe of meeting Carter. Reg offered a nervous hand for CS to shake, stuttering, "I... I'm a huge fan, Mr Stone. Read all your books."

"Good to meet you, Reg, Mertle. Remind me to autograph a book for you before you leave."

Reg blushed with gratitude.

"Please sit down," Denise said warmly, "tell us what you witnessed?"

They exchanged a glance for Mertle to do the talking. "Well, we'd just finished the tour of CBS—it was high on our list of points of visitation..." Reg nudged her not to drift; she got the hint and continued more succinct. "We were outside the Broadcast Center when out of nowhere comes this motorbike aiming right for her, the girl, crossing 57th Street... well if that bike didn't hit her and then, to our shock and horror, it just sped off..."

"A hit and run," Reg added.

"Oh, it was just terrible. Anyhow, that's what I saw; Reg was busy taking photos... it's his hobby, you know, taking photos. Anyhow, when Mr Stone ran out onto the road and yelled for us to call an ambulance, and I ran inside CBS and got them to telephone one."

CS was sitting on the end of his desk. He stubbed out his cigarette in the ashtray, "And thank God you did, Mertle; I'd say you saved the girl's life."

It was Mertle's turn to blush. "How is she, Mr Stone, the girl. Do you know?"

"A broken neck, sadly she'll probably never walk again, only twenty-three, poor lass," CS said with compassion.

Mertle and Reg exchanged looks of concern, and Mertle said, "Oh dear, that is dreadful."

"I used my motor drive SLR to capture the accident... and I got something odd. Which is why we came to you, Mr Stone."

Mertle smiled, "Reg recognised you."

Reg produced a yellow packet of 8 x 10 prints from his inside coat pocket and handed them one at a time to CS. He studied each picture, grimacing, and then passed them to Denise. They looked through half a dozen, but Reg held onto the last one.

"This is the odd one I spoke of. I tried to get a shot of the bike hightailing it up the street, and this is what I got."

He handed the print to CS. The photo showed the bike driving up a ramp into the rear of a parked removalist truck. CS handed it to Denise.

"Confirmation it was a hit and run... and for me, with intent," CS said sternly.

Mertle piped up, "Should we take these to the police?"

"Absolutely," CS was adamant.

"I got double prints... so you can keep a copy," Reg affirmed.

"Excellent, Reg," CS said, getting up and fetching a book from his desktop.

"How long are you in town?" Denise asked.

"We take the train tonight, well, the train actually goes to Nashville, we're staying there a day or two then we'll take the Greyhound home to Bowling Green, Kentucky; it's only sixty miles there," Mertle said, not shy of taking the opportunity to make a statement into a short story.

CS autographed the inside cover of the book and handed it to Reg. "There you go, Reg; have you read "The Underpants Killer?""

"No... no, very much appreciated, Mr Stone," Reg said thankfully, studying the cover shot of a buxom blonde lass in a white bikini with a pair of men's boxer shorts over her head.

"Call me CS, Reg," CS said, holding out his hand to shake and ending the meeting. He'd done so many meet and greets at book signings over the years he had become a master of closing a chat down.

Denise was also an expert, his co-conspirator, standing and then making for the door. "Thank you for taking the time."

Reg stood, "Will we be reading about the bike accident in your next book, CS?"

"You'll have to buy a copy to find that out, Reg," CS chuckled flippantly.

Denise saw them out, then after closing the door, returned to CS, who was studying the photo with a magnifying glass.

"I see Dumbo Removals, Brooklyn on the side of the truck and… a licence plate," he said jotting it down.

Denise was on it in a flash… flicked through the telephone book. "Got it. Surely the perps couldn't be that stupid, could they?"

"Don't think they were expecting to be photographed. We need to beat the cops to them. Let's move," CS said, heading for the door.

CHAPTER SEVEN

The Dumbo Archway, Brooklyn. The Stones got out of a taxi on Water Street and walked into the Archway. On the other side were the docks, Anchorage Place, and the offices of Dumbo Removals. They crossed the street and entered the front office.

Denise checked the young receptionist's name tag, then said courteously, "Hi Eisha, I hope you can help me... Can I contact the driver of this truck of yours?" She handed her the licence number on a slip of paper.

Reading it, the young girl said, "It's my first day at work; I don't know."

Denise advised conspiratorially, "You could just check the manifest."

Eisha reluctantly opened a book on the countertop.

"Oh, it's not one of ours, I mean, it is, but it's a rental, um, not our driver."

"I see, so can you tell me who to contact, you see, he forgot something."

"Sure, it's the Libyan Consulate."

A big guy burst into the office, furious. His name-tag read Ajeeb Bashir, Manager.

He scolded the young girl, "Eisha, never disclose the identity of our customer to strangers."

Distressed, Eisha apologised, "Yes, uncle, so sorry."

Ajeeb irreverently pushed her aside further chastising her in a foreign language.

"I'm sorry, Mr Bashir," Denise apologised, stopping his tirade. "I didn't mean to cause any trouble for Eisha."

"Can't help," he snapped angrily. "Leave your number, and I'll pass it on… All I can do."

"That's all right, thank you."

Denise didn't leave a number, and Ajeeb evil-eyed them as they left.

Outside, CS hailed a taxi.

"I didn't like Bashir's vibe," Denise admitted.

They hopped into the taxi. CS directed the driver, "City morgue."

~ ~ ~

Thirty-four years younger with a shock of black curly hair, Booker, garbed in a mortuary attendant's blue gown, slid a corpse into a mortuary cabinet. CS and Denise entered.

"I was wondering how long it would take before you two showed up. The horse arm case, right?"

"Right-on," CS crowed.

"Booker," Denise said warmly, "how are you, darling?" Gave him a friendly hug.

"I'm all good, but you know while it's an active case, I'm restricted—"

"Oh, just a little peek, pretty please?" Denise said using her charm.

"My favourite crime writers always get their way with me."

CS tapped an unfiltered cigarette on his thumbnail and lit it. Looked about at the toe-tagged bodies on slabs. Booker went to a mortuary cabinet and opened it.

"You've been busy."

Sliding out the drawer, Booker said, "You know CS, there are always more murders on a full moon." He waved them over to view the severed arm.

"You can see it was severed by a sharp instrument, a meat cleaver I'd say."

CS got real close to it, "Yes, I think you're right Book. Hmm, check this out." He pointed to a mark on the limb. Booker and Denise closed in on it.

"What is that?" Booker questioned.

"I have a similar mark on my arm after having a tattoo removed. Leaves a thin white outline," CS said.

Denise nodded, "It's probably the cyanosis that now makes it visible."

"You're right," CS agreed, "forensics would have missed it for sure."

"It's definitely not on the report and hell, I didn't see it," Booker admitted contritely.

"You got a magnifying glass, Book?" CS asked.

Booker produced one from a drawer and handed it to CS. He looked through at the tattoo and then handed the glass to Denise.

"It's the emblem of the Hermetic Order of the Golden Dawn," CS said.

Denise looked up at him, "Not only that but it's the New York chapter."

"Shit, girl, how'd you know that?" Booker asked intrigued.

"We're both members," CS said handing the glass to Booker.

He peered at the tattoo through it and muttered, "Well, I'll be."

~ ~ ~

Back at the office, Denise was at her computer typing with CS standing behind her smoking.

"So what do we have so far?" CS asked.

Denise sat back in her chair and reported, "Well, suspects: none really. It is feasible that the hit and run on Liz Parks had something to do with the Libyan Consulate, but we need motive. The arm possibly belonged to a member of the Golden Dawn, and I've not yet heard anything back from Detective Joe Blake."

CS exhaled a column of smoke. "And then there's old bad-vibes Ajeeb Bashir." He grumbled while skilfully rotating a pencil between his fingers.

"Finding the murderer is predicated on determining motive."

CS nodded thoughtfully, "Yes my dear, I think that needs to be our focus."

"You know CS, you can't just go around with all the bravado of one of your detective characters... this is for real, darling... these perps are playing for keeps."

"I hear you," he said gently, resting a loving hand on her shoulder. "I don't have the authority or the bravado of my protagonists; however, we do have their logic."

Denise covered his hand with hers. "Darling, you could get yourself killed."

~ ~ ~

I was rotating a pencil between my fingers while Kendy looked up from her laptop.

"We're pretty much in the same position," I said.

"Except we have the murder of Liz Parks, and like a plausible motive."

"True, I need to speak with this Joe Blake."

"What are you going to do about Rixon? He wants the disk?"

"He can't have it until we have what we want from it."

"There's really no point in doing much more investigating ourselves when all the answers could be like in the data," Kendy said.

I thought out loud, "Only difference is Liz's death... I'm not sure the news footage is a strong enough motive to get her killed."

"Unless..." Kendy said, having a Eureka moment, "What if, like, there's someone in the footage that doesn't want to be recognised?"

I froze with the revelation. "Right-on Kendy. You're absolutely on the money, and we know CBS has the footage because I saw it on the box this morning. Okay, make copies of the data. Hide them on the cloud. Keep reading.and take notes; we need to know if they ID'd the arm. I'm going to CBS."

I left Kendy to continue reading my mother's story.

In 1988, CS sat on a Chesterfield lounge in the main office of the Golden Dawn Society, engaged in conversation with Colonel George Witten, USAF Retired, who occupied an armchair opposite. George, in his early 70s, possessed regal features, complete with a bushy white handlebar moustache.

"You're saying there was a tattoo of the Golden Dawn on this arm that had been removed?" the Colonel exclaimed, his pronounced southern accent reflecting his astonishment.

"Yes, Colonel, you could clearly see the outline, and furthermore, it was the New York chapter," CS affirmed.

"Then you'd have to expect he was or is a member of the lodge."

"Indeed. I was thinking we might be able to narrow it down by determining if a member is missing."

"Hmm, there's that analytical mind of yours ticking away, CS; excellent thinking. You know, membership renewal was due this month; we could see who hasn't paid."

The Colonel lifted the telephone receiver from the table beside him and spoke, "Dorris, can you bring me the membership dues ledger?" He put down the receiver and topped up CS's glass with JD, then his own. CS tapped a cigarette on his thumbnail and lit up. The Colonel followed suit.

"A loathsome thing being butchered like that. You'd have to think there was serious motive."

Dorris waddled in, chewing gum like a tumble dryer. Her curly blonde hair was worn up, red lipstick, lilac business suit with big shoulder pads; she was in sharp contrast to her 19th Century surroundings. She handed the Colonel the ledger, then waddled back out. CS's eyeline followed her all the way out. He was fascinated by her.

"You know Dorris would make an excellent character in one of my stories."

The Colonel raised his bushy eyebrows. "Yes-sirree, she sure would... Now, let me see here... aha, aside from you and Mrs Stone having not paid, there are six others." CS grimaced at being caught out. After a pause to let the obligation sink in, the Colonel continued. "We can eliminate three of them; two are women, and the third is in a nursing home with dementia. That leaves Anthony Cornish, Major Hercules Wayne, Retired, and Daniel Anderson. Is that at all helpful?"

CS skulled his drink. "If I can have their contacts, it would make it easier to chase them up."

Witten pulled a gold fountain pen from his inside coat pocket, jotted down the details on a notepad, ripped out the page, and handed it to CS. "There you go... y'all let me know if I can be of any further assistance, CS."

They stood and shook hands.

"I'll do that, Colonel... and I will attend to those outstanding fees."

~ ~ ~

At her office desk, Kendy answered her phone. "Hello, baby. Yes, the files opened beautifully; you're a genius. Dinner! Um, I'd love to. What's on the menu? Me! Tell me about it...?"

Sitting and waiting at reception in the CBS News Room, my ringtone, "The Terrible Tango," alerted me. "Rixon. No, I don't have the disk. Man, you need anger management." Rixon terminated the call. I put away my phone.

~ ~ ~

Kendy was facing the office window, engaged in conversation with Dwip over the phone. The setting sun cast long shadows across the room. "Grandma will be there... Okay, six o'clock... can't wait. Mwah, love you." She put away her phone, about to turn away from the window, when suddenly, a hand holding a knife whipped around her neck from behind. The blade pressed against her throat, drawing blood, and Kendy panicked.

"The disk or I will cut your throat," demanded the assailant, his voice muffled by a balaclava.

~ ~ ~

1988:

CS stepped out onto the pavement from the Golden Dawn Building in Hell's Kitchen. Headlights flashing on him from the traffic, he heads west on 53rd toward 6th Avenue, hunting for a taxi. There are few pedestrians. Sound alerts him to someone tailing him. He stops abruptly. So does the tail. Confirmed. He starts walking at a faster pace, then he notices a car keeping pace with him, and so darts across 53rd. His tail copies. The car stops up ahead of him, and a guy gets out and then waits suspiciously on the sidewalk. He can hear the tail's footsteps speed up. With his heart pumping, CS knows he's being pushed into a pincer movement, sees a taxi. He almost jumps in front of it to flag it down, hops in.

As the cab moves with the traffic, CS looks out the window. His tail meets up with the guy on the pavement; they both get into the waiting car. CS swivels to look out the back window. The car is in pursuit of them.

"Fifty bucks to lose the car tailing us."

"No problem, buddy," the driver replied with a Brooklyn accent.

~ ~ ~

I opened the door, and darkness enveloped the room, broken intermittently by the flashing blue neon from across the street. As I reached for the light switch, my foot collided with something on the floor, and it emitted a muffled yelp. Flicking on the light, I discovered Kendy hogtied and gagged.

"Kendy!" I rushed to untie her, and she sat up, clutching her throat.

"He threatened to slit my throat," she choked out, her eyes filled with fear.

I helped her to her feet and gave her a comforting hug. Tears welled up in her eyes as she began to sob.

"Take it easy, come, sit down, and tell me what happened."

She picked up her smashed phone from the floor and asked if she could use mine to text Dwip. I handed her my phone, and she sent a quick message to let her friend know she was safe, albeit shaken.

"It's okay. Did you get a good look at him?"

As she wiped away tears, she began to describe her attacker. "He was about your height, smelled of tobacco, and he only had half a pinky on his right hand. He wore a black balaclava."

"Well, that rules out Rixon. Sit down; you still look wobbly."

Kendy took a seat on the couch and continued her account. "He only spoke once, and he had an accent. Oh, before he attacked me, I read some more of the book. CS had two guys tailing him when he left the Golden Dawn. He managed to like lose them. He got the names of three possible owners of the arm who hadn't paid their membership fees. That's where I got up to... then I got a call from Dwip. I was standing at the window talking to her when he must've come in and crept up behind me."

"So that's as far as you got with the book?"

"Yeah, I've been on the floor tied up for the last two hours. Did you get the tape?"

I held up a flash drive. "Do fish swim? Come on, I'll walk you to Dwip's."

~ ~ ~

I accompanied Kendy to Dwip's apartment block in Lower Manhattan. She stopped me at the entrance.

"This is it, thanks, boss."

"Do you live here as well?"

"No, no, just up the street. No, I'm having dinner with my

girlfriend, Dwip."

"The computer Nerd… I thought Dwip was a guy. All good, enjoy your evening, see you in the A.M."

Watching her safely inside, I decided to make a call. I dialled the number and waited for the person on the other end to pick up.

"Hey, Axis Stone here… thought you might like to—"

CHAPTER EIGHT

I had nodded off on the couch when the door buzzer jolted me awake. Knowing who it would be, I made a frantic effort to tidy up the apartment. On the fly, I pressed the entry button on the intercom, then issued an order, "Siri, play seduction one."

Barry White's Love Theme began playing at the same time as a knock sounded at the door. I danced over to the door, stopped, sniffed my armpits—they were fine—and opened the door. On the other side stood lovely Lisa, the librarian from the Golden Dawn.

"Well, look at you, Lisa, a vision, living up to the promise," I remarked.

"Yes, well, I felt good about coming tonight," she purred with a hint of innuendo.

"Come in, you may. You've found the right guy and the right place."

She breezed past me, grinning smugly and dressed ravishingly.

"And Barry White to boot!" she cackled.

I motioned for her to sit on the couch. "Siri, lower the volume. Now Lisa, what can I get to wet your whistle?"

"Whatever you're having will be fine."

My cellarette was well-stocked. I went to it and returned with a bottle of red and two glasses. I showed her the label. "A very special wine, the 2014 Kaesler Old Bastard Shiraz. I brought it with me from Australia for a special occasion, and this is it."

"Hmm, lucky me. You're from there, aren't you?"

I opened the wine and poured two glasses. "Yep, born there, raised here until I was seven, and then back to Aussie for my education. Only recently came back here."

I handed her a glass, and we touched glasses in a toast before taking a sip.

"Jeremy said you're a PI, an interesting profession."

"It has its ups and downs."

"Hmm," she licked her sensuous full lips, "now that's what I like to hear."

~ ~ ~

Later, we were sitting up in bed. Lisa was without her glasses, her hair was messed up, and she looked like she had been through a torrid encounter.

With bedroom blue eyes, she said, "So, did you find what you were looking for?"

"What are we talking about now?" I joked. "Did Jeremy tell you?"

"Yes, he needed to explain the missing file."

"Of course. Are you a member of the Golden Dawn?"

"Aha," she confirmed.

"And what does that entail?"

She snuggled up against me cutely. "Just like any fellowship... like-minded folk who prefer to sidestep the dominion of emotional cripples and patriotic fools."

"By engaging in Hermetic mysticism?"

"You make it sound like a disease."

"Sorry, I didn't mean to be patronising..."

"You should join... your parents were members."

"I think that was for research. They wrote a number of books using occultism, like 'The Pagan Rite' and 'Which Witch,' among others."

"The Golden Dawn is more about metaphysics, the paranormal, a magical order rather than witchcraft, with three orders of teaching.

Women have equal standing."

"And which order are you?"

"Second order, focusing on divination, astral projection, and alchemy."

"Right. So, where are the main lodges?"

"As well as here, in Canada, the UK, South Africa, Australia, Sweden, France, the Middle East, and India... among others."

"South Africa, that's interesting."

"Sir Arthur Conan Doyle, Bram Stoker, William Yeats, the famous suffragette Maud Gonne, all members. You'd be surprised by the notoriety of members, even today..."

~ ~ ~

The next morning, I found Kendy at her computer. She looked up and beamed me an uplifting smile. "Good morning, boss. Just got in myself. You look as though you had a big one?"

"A little rough around the edges. Too many reds. Let's look at this," I said, tossing her a flash-drive. She caught it and inserted it into her laptop.

We watched the unedited footage of the time-coded 1988 Liz Parks Pier 25 news report. It opened with Liz on screen, preparing herself for the live take. A crowd of around fifteen people were gathered in the background, looking down at something on the deck. Three fingers appeared in close-up to countdown: three, two, one.

In mid-shot, holding a CBS News microphone, Liz reported, "I'm at Pier 25, and let me tell you, this is the most bizarre case. A recreational fisherman made a catch he didn't expect in the Hudson River today: the torso of a horse. You heard me, the body of a horse in the Hudson River in the middle of downtown New York. And get this; it had a severed human arm sewn into its belly." She walked into the crowd, which moved aside for her. The camera tilted down to show the gruesome sight of the torso of a dead horse with its belly cut open. Liz continued in voiceover. "The police removed the severed arm for forensic examination... but look at this thing..." The camera tilted up to her in mid-shot. "So, the question remains: where's the rest of the missing person? Liz Parks for CBS News."

Kendy hit the space bar to freeze the footage and said, "I didn't notice anything strange, did you?"

"Actually, I did. At twenty-two seconds, can you grab a screenshot?"

Kendy rewound the footage to the mark, froze it, and then took a screenshot. She opened the JPEG.

"See the guy facing the camera trying to obscure his face with his hand? Now roll the footage and watch what he does."

Kendy rolled the footage. The guy obscuring his face ducked, then quickly moved through the crowd like he was trying to escape the camera.

"So, who is Mr Guilty?"

"I think we're looking at a motive for murder. This, I reckon, is the second man… Liz had said three dudes had requested a dub that day, Rixon, then the guy that looked Middle Eastern, who she gave the bum's rush to, and then Dad."

"Yeah, that could definitely be the Middle Eastern guy hiding his face. Who is he?"

"That's for us to find out," I said.

"Why is all this happening now, after all these years?"

"Good question, but the answer is probably that we've opened a can of worms… Let's carry on with 'The Last Word.'"

Kendy opened the document, and I read from where she'd left off.

"After the Hell's Kitchen scare, I tried to talk CS out of pursuing the case any further… but trying to talk CS out of anything is like head-butting a brick wall."

~ ~ ~

1988: With his feet up on his office desk, puffing on a cigarette, CS was on the phone, following up on the leads from the Golden Dawn.

~ ~ ~

In his fifties with a receding hairline, wearing a bright floral Hawaiian shirt, Anthony picked up the ringing telephone receiver and asked, "Hello?"

"Is that Anthony Cornish?" CS asked.

"It is indeed."

"My name is Axis Stone, I'm just ringing to remind you that your dues for the Golden Dawn are overdue."

He chuckled light-heartedly, "Um, cheque's in the mail."

"Oh, and might I ask, do you have both arms?"

"Last time I checked."

"Thank you," CS said, ending the call.

~ ~ ~

Cornish wasn't armless, so that took him out of the equation. He dialled Major Hercules Wayne, but there was no answer. He called out to Denise in her office.

"No answer from Major Wayne. It says here he's got one of those newfangled portable phones."

"Try it," came her response.

~ ~ ~

Well-built for his sixties, Major Wayne, with a Havana cigar clenched between his teeth, was about to tee off at Sleepy Willow Country Club in New York. Just as he was swinging, the sound of his phone ringing caused him to duff the shot. Disgruntled, puffing the cigar like a steam engine, he strode over to retrieve his phone from the golf cart. The size of a house brick, he had to extend the aerial.

He answered irritably. "This better be good. Who is it? Oh, yes… I know the name… of course, I've read your books. No, I'm on a golfing tour with my wife. Haven't I? Well, I'll have my secretary attend to that immediately. Pass on my apologies to Colonel George. Thank you, Stone."

By now, his wife was getting set to tee off.

"Guess who that was, Carls?" the major said, striding back to the tee.

Carl was placing the ball on the tee. "No idea."

"The novelist, Carter Stone."

Unimpressed, she took her shot, and it was a good one.

~ ~ ~

CS dialled the last number, waited, and then hung up. He called out to Denise, "Another one bites the dust... that's it." He made his way into her office.

Still typing on her computer, she stopped and looked up at him. "No luck, huh, hon?"

He massaged her shoulders. "This guy, Daniel Anderson, lives in Astoria, Queens. I think we should pay him a visit... I have a gut feeling."

~ ~ ~

Trusting that gut feeling, CS and Denise hailed a yellow Chevrolet Impala taxi to Queens. The taxi pulled up outside a strawberry-coloured three-story apartment block.

CS pressed the buzzer to Apartment 202. Nothing. After a couple more tries, he pressed the manager button, 203.

After a moment, a loud Yiddish accent answered, "Yes, 'ello, who's there?"

"Good afternoon, ma'am. Can I speak with you about Mr Daniel Anderson?"

"Who is that? Don't want to buy nothing."

"Your next-door neighbour, ma'am."

"No, you're not, he's not here. Go 'way."

"Wait, I just need to ask you about him."

"Oh, one moment, I'm coming down."

CS smiled blandly at Denise, who chuckled at the old lady's

retort. CS was just lighting up a cigarette when the door opened to reveal a small, hunched lady with a walking stick, well into her 80s.

"Are you relatives? What has he done?"

Denise answered courteously, "No, and nothing."

The blue rinsed, silver-haired old lady cuffed her ear and barked, "What's that? Speak up, dear, don't speak in riddles."

Denise couldn't help but giggle. "We need to speak to Daniel about a family matter."

"Oh, you're an attorney. He hasn't been there for days, was wondering about the cats, he has three of them, you know?"

Denise quickly changed her tack, "Yes, we're here to check on them."

"Oh, good. Then you better come in then. Someone needs to check."

She turned and hobbled off along the dim hallway. They followed, having to walk slower than they would normally, then up a rickety staircase to the 2nd floor, along another dim, dank hallway.

"He paid a year in advance, you know? Unusual that. Since Ezra passed away two years ago, I've had to manage the place on my own," she said, talking to Denise and CS behind her. She stopped at Room 202, fumbled with a keyring of keys, found the right one, and opened the door. They were immediately hit by a foul stench that forced them to cover their noses.

"Phew, something's dead in there," CS said.

"I can't smell anything, it's my sinuses..." Mrs Goldstein said.

Denise and CS, pinching their noses, followed her into the Spartan room. It was just a living room, a kitchenette, one bedroom, and a bathroom. A cat ran up to Denise and brushed around her legs. Denise picked her up. The obnoxious smell led them to the kitchen, where they found two half-eaten cats on the floor, bloated with maggots.

"Oh, how gross... She had to eat the other two," Denise said.

"Oy, gevalt!" Mrs Goldstein yelped.

Denise and CS exchanged a sly sign for her to keep Mrs Goldstein talking while he reconnoitred the bedroom.

The bed was tidy, not slept in. There was a suitcase on the floor. He checked the tag on the handle: JNB/JFK SA. He ripped it off and pocketed it. He opened the top drawer of the bedside table and found a gun. Pocketed it.

"Well?" Mrs Goldstein snapped while standing in the doorway, with a cat in her arms glaring at him. "

On the back seat of a taxi, Denise asked, "So, what did you unearth?"

CS handed her the tag. "This might tell us something; it was on a suitcase."

Denise studied it. "JNB is Johannesburg, and SA is South African Airways. There's a date, May 4, 1988, four months ago."

"She said he paid a year in advance. Pity I couldn't find a passport, not enough time."

"Maybe he's South African?"

"Time for some serious research, my love. We might just have the person that matches the arm. By the way, why are we going East on 48th Street?"

Denise smiled at her husband, "To buy Joe Blake lunch. Stop here, driver."

~ ~ ~

The Hatsuhana Sushi Restaurant was packed with lunchtime patrons. Denise spoke to the host at the front desk. As they were led to a reserved table, CS asked, "Tell me why we are meeting him?"

"To talk. This is his favourite lunchtime haunt. Let's order some hot Sake," Denise said excitedly.

Looking his scruffiest, unkempt hair, stubble, suit in need of a good dry-cleaning, Joe was at the table.

"Hey, Joe, this is my husband, Carter Stone," Denise said by way of introduction.

Blake's expression was sullen. CS held out his hand, and they shook. Blake lit up a cigarette with a Zippo lighter. CS waited for

Denise to sit, then took a seat and lit up his own cigarette. He sized Blake up: mid-forties, five nine, Latino or Italian heritage, been around the traps.

"I've read a couple of your books," Blake said. "The Little Sister and A Fraction too much Friction."

"Friction was mine, but the Little Sister is Raymond Chandler, I think."

"Oh yeah, so it was Philip Marlowe. Your PI had too high of an opinion of himself for my liking."

"Yeah, I wrote Danny that way. Can't please everyone—"

Denise cut in before the conversation could sour. "Why don't you order for us, Joe? You must know the menu."

"No problem," Blake growled. "Drinks?"

"Hot sake would be great," Denise said, licking her red-painted lips.

While Blake ordered, CS told Denise on the sly, "He doesn't like my detective... Think I should ask him about Anderson?"

"We wanted to know how the police investigation is proceeding," Denise asked Blake.

Blake pulled a 'you're wasting my time' face and replied, "Look, if you're here to talk about the horse arm case, then forget it, it's closed. Capiche."

CS inquired, "What do you mean closed? Is it solved?"

The waiter arrived and filled three ceramic cups with Sake. Blake nodded to him, then answered CS. "No, closed is closed. End of story."

"Why?" Denise questioned.

"Don't ask me, I'm just a cop. It's in the hands of the USSS, FBI, the CIA—"

Denise cut him off, shrugging her shoulders at CS. "The USSS, that's the presidential secret service?"

"What the hell would they have to do with it? Look, we think we know the identity of the victim."

"He who belongs to the said arm? Tell them, not me. I'm officially off the case."

"Is there anything you can offer to help us with our inquiries, Joe?" Denise asked.

Blake held up his cup of Sake. "Yeah. Konpai."

The Stones copied in toast, "Konpai."

After a sip, Blake growled, "My advice to you, is, drop it."

Denise couldn't believe it. "Don't you feel guilty leaving it unsolved?"

"I don't do guilt."

CS piped up, "Then answer me one question..." The food arrived. "Does the name Daniel Anderson mean anything to you?"

Blake stubbed out his cigarette in the ashtray and then started eating. While chewing on a sushi roll, he looked at CS and grumbled, "No."

"Do me a favour?"

"Depends, you said you had only one question."

"This isn't a TV quiz show, Blake. This fellow Daniel Anderson has been missing for several days; we think it was his arm. We went to his apartment today, the landlord let us in, I found a gun in a drawer. This is the serial number." He handed over a piece of paper.

Blake took it and read it. "AFT can only check if it's been used in a crime or stolen. Don't recognise the number, means it's probably military or Feds."

CHAPTER NINE

The office was the scene of an argument. Denise was unhappy with her husband's reluctance to recognise the dangers of the case.

"You're being obstinate," she told him. "Blake was warding us off the case for a reason, don't you get that?"

Carter Stone was pacing his office while Denise was arguing from hers.

He appealed, "Denise…"

"Oh, here we go," she snapped. "Whenever you call me Denise, you're not going to listen to me."

He pleaded, "If we accept defeat based on one person's opinion, then we're not doing our job."

"Job?" she squealed angrily. "Our job is writing books, mate. Our job is staying alive to raise our son."

Carter went to her, took her hand, and appealed, "Look, this South African connection has me intrigued. Just let me pursue one last line of inquiry. Please?"

She weakened, "Hmm, and what's that?"

"I'll go back to Colonel George at the Golden Dawn for more info on Daniel Anderson. If that gets us nowhere, then I'll drop it like a hot potato, I promise."

She nodded grudgingly. "Just remember last time you were there, you were tailed."

He beamed her a big smile and then lovingly kissed her on the lips.

Carrying a bouquet of flowers, Denise entered a hospital room at New York-Presbyterian. In the bed, in traction, with her neck in a brace, was Liz Parks. Denise placed the flowers in a vase on the bedside table.

"Hello, Liz. I'm Denise Stone, the wife of Carter. I came to see how you're getting on and if you need anything."

With teary eyes, Liz answered, "Doctors say I'll never walk again."

Denise sat on the edge of the bed and gently took Liz's hand. "Oh dear, keep the faith, love, never say never."

Liz began to sob. "I've lost my job. It was a hit and run, so no third-party insurance, and now the police have dropped the case. I don't know what to do..."

"We'll help you, love. We're still on the case. Have you had any visitors?"

"Only the guy from the FBI... He came to talk about the horse arm case but wasn't interested in the hit and run. I don't like him at all."

"Doesn't he see the connection?"

"No, and neither do I," she protested.

Denise gently squeezed her hand supportively. "What did he ask you?"

"Dumb stuff like, did I see anything unusual while I was at Pier 25?"

"Hmm, you told my husband that two others asked you for a dub of the news footage that day. Was this FBI guy one of them?"

"Yeah, he came first. That's right, his name is Rixon, Agent Rixon."

"Do you think he got a copy of the footage?"

"Yes, but not from me. Why? How do you think it's connected?"

"We think there must be someone in the footage who doesn't want to be recognised. Who can I see at CBS to get a copy or to view it?"

"You won't be able to; he told me the FBI sequestered everything."

~ ~ ~

Carter Stone and Colonel George sat in armchairs in the Colonel's office, smoking and drinking coffee.

"That's dang terrible!" the Colonel exclaimed. "So, you think the cat fed on the other two?"

"Cannibal cat. Would make a good book title," Carter remarked. "Thing-of-it-is, Anderson strikes me as being odd. Is there anything more you'd have on him here?"

"We could check his profile. I mean, it'd be nothing special, only general membership details, referees, and so forth. I'll ask Dorris."

He pressed a button on the phone beside him to summon Dorris. After a moment or two, the door opened, and in she came dressed in a pink cardigan, a pale blue blouse, a white mini skirt, and white sandals.

Chewing gum, she asked, "Yeah, Colonel, sup?"

"Can you bring me the profile and whatever else we have on member Daniel Anderson, please?"

She nodded and then waddled out past Carter, shooting him a not-so-sly wink. The Colonel caught the wink and raised an eyebrow. Carter noticed his reaction and, looking guilty, cleared his throat.

"When you say odd...?" the Colonel questioned.

"Oh, his Spartan living conditions... The apartment was not lived in at all; he's even a mystery to his landlady. He arrived here from—"

He stopped, enamoured by the arrival of Dorris with a folder. She bent down to hand it to the Colonel, glancing amorously at Carter while showing off her shapely legs. A little moment transpired between her and Carter. She straightened up and peered at him and then said suggestively Marilyn Monroe-like, "Anything else?"

"No thank you, Dorris," the Colonel said, cognizant of the flirtatious little number going on. He took a deep breath, used to it.

"You were saying?"

"He's from—"

Reading the file, the Colonel finished the sentence for him. "Johannesburg, South Africa. Yes, says here he's with the NIS, that's the National Intelligence Service there."

Carter crossed his legs and nodded, it was good intel. "Aha, the enforcers of apartheid."

"Yes, nasty stuff that. Only other reference is to his visits to other chapters such as Windhoek Namibia, London, Stockholm, here— that's about it. Oh, he was originally nominated for membership in Stockholm."

"Stockholm, really? By whom?"

"Let's see here, ah, a Bengt Nilsson, hmm, the Assistant Secretary of the UN, Commissioner for Namibia."

Carter was impressed. "High profile... maybe Anderson was a spy for the NIS, and that's what got him killed?"

"Assuming it was his arm, and that he's dead."

"Well, he has been missing three days. Found this in his bedside drawer." He pulled a pistol from his inside coat pocket and handed it to George.

After checking it, he said, "Hmm, judging by the serial number, it's not military but might well belong to a federal agency."

It was the same as what Joe Blake had told him. "FBI or CIA, interesting."

~ ~ ~

With Anderson's gun in his hand, CS paced the floor of his office, smoking like a train. Denise watched him and listened intently.

CS stopped and held up the gun. "So, this is FBI or CIA. Anderson is South African, a spy for the NIS... has friends in high places."

"This fellow Bengt Nilsson?"

"Yes, UN Assistant Secretary-General and UN Commissioner for Namibia."

"Namibia, Anderson went there as well, didn't he?"

"Yes, to the capital Windhoek."

"I wonder what's going on there that might have attracted his attention?" Denise thought out loud.

CS studied the gun in his hand again and then put it in his pocket. "You look into Namibia and Nilsson. So… Liz said she had a visit from Rixon, who'd sequestered the footage from CBS. I need to get him on the horn."

He moved behind his desk while Denise went into her office. As CS reached for the phone, it rang.

"Hello. Yes, Dorris, slow down… tell me what happened from when I left."

She explained, "I was at my desk checking my lipstick in my compact mirror. I got up to go to the bathroom. When I came back from the bathroom, two burglars came rushing out of the Colonel's office toward me. I froze… I was petrified. One of them thumped me in the nose, and I hit the deck… on purpose, so they couldn't do any more damage. They got away. I got up, my nose was broken and bleeding, but I wanted to see if the Colonel was all right. I found him on the floor… felt for a pulse, and then dialled 911. I saw your calling card on the desk, so I phoned you."

"Has an ambulance arrived?"

"Paramedics are here now."

"Can you ask them the Colonel's condition?"

"Cardiac arrest… they're taking him to hospital now," Dorris said.

"Okay, call me." He hung up and glared at Denise, who was waiting in anticipation of bad news. "That was Dorris, Colonel Witten's secretary at the Golden Dawn; they were assaulted just after I left."

She was shocked. "Oh dear, how are they?"

"She has a broken nose, and the Colonel suffered a heart attack. They're being taken to the hospital. Who the hell is doing this?"

"Was it a robbery or what?"

"She said all they took was Anderson's membership profile folder."

Denise flopped onto the couch. CS turned his back on her and stared out of the window into the setting sun.

"I don't like this," Denise said gravely.

"It all connects." He turned to face her. "You see, the bike wasn't meant to hit Liz, the rider was supposed to snatch the tape. They knew she had it and was going to give it to me. How? Because Liz told me when the second fellow turned up, just before I did, also wanting a dub, in her own words, she had given him the bum's rush. But she didn't call security. So, when I stepped out of the elevator on the News Room floor, I could've literally walked right past him, but I didn't, I saw no-one."

He was now pacing the floor with Denise watching him like she was in the audience at Wimbledon, seated at the net, watching the ball during a tennis final.

"So… let's speculate that he saw me and then quickly slipped into a vacant cubicle. I meet Liz, and we talked. As she's walking me out after only a few minutes later, we closed a deal: I'd pay her, and she'd deliver me the tape on 57th Street fifteen minutes later. He had to have overheard us, picked up the phone on the desk in the cubicle, and quietly arranged for an accomplice, the biker, to snatch the tape from Liz."

He sat on the edge of his desk, proud of his deduction, and lit a cigarette.

Denise took over pacing. "But why?" she questioned.

He thought a moment before answering, "They must have needed it to verify if one of their agents had been exposed in it or not, it's the only logical explanation."

~ ~ ~

I stopped reading and told Kendy, "I think we need to look into a few names… anything could have happened between 1988 and now. We'll start with this dude Daniel Anderson."

Kendy Googled him. "There's nothing on him. I think we need to find out what happened when CS meets up with Rixon."

"Yes, you're probably right."
I resumed reading the manuscript.

~ ~ ~

Denise was unpacking a new gadget that was all the rage, a facsimile machine. "This'll make it a lot easier to work with our book cover artists," she said to CS, who was at his desk deep in thought.

The phone rang, he answered. "Hello, yes, this is he… Oh, thank you for getting back to me," he checked his wristwatch, "yes, that'll be fine."

"Who was that?" Denise asked.

"FBI agent Jake Rixon, we'll meet up at Café Wha! at six."

"Better get going then, it's past five."

He was one step ahead of her. He snatched his coat, gave her a peck on the cheek, and then flew out the door bound for Greenwich Village.

As he stepped out of the cab, CS checked the gathering of hip young people out front of Café Wha! 'Voodoo Child' by Jimi Hendrix playing inside was loud enough to hear out there.

Inside the bar was crowded, all the tables loaded, the small stage unoccupied, 'Voodoo Child' was blaring. The walls were decorated with rock posters and framed photos of famous rock bands and rock icons of the '60s, '70s, and '80s. The lighting was dim. CS felt right out of place, more like a Wall Street broker than a punter. He worked his way to the bar and ordered a drink. As it arrived, he noticed a couple leave a table, so he took it.

CHAPTER
TEN

Rixon entered Café Wha!, paused inside the door, and surveyed the room. He was dressed in the classic attire of a federal agent: a black suit, white shirt, and a slim black tie. He spotted CS, navigated his way over, and pulled up a chair.

"His excellency Carter Stone," he stated facetiously, raising his voice above Hendrix's music.

"Flattered you hold me in such high esteem, Rixon," CS retorted with a touch of sarcasm, always ready for a verbal duel. "Drink?"

"I'll take a coke. I'm on duty."

CS caught the attention of a waitress and placed the order.

"It seems we just missed each other at CBS the other day."

CS sensed a defensive shift in Rixon's body language. "Yes, and I heard you rescued a distressed damsel."

In a more sombre tone, CS replied, "I'd use a more descriptive word than 'distressed,' Rixon: the girl's life has been ruined. It's a shame you're not actively pursuing her attacker."

"I would expect better word choice from an author, Stone, but that doesn't change the facts. It's out of my hands. It's up to the police."

"So, why would the CBS news footage be of interest to you, enough to have it removed and then bury the case?"

"And why is that any of your business? Don't tell me this is going to be one of your trashy paperbacks?"

"We can't all have class, Rixon. It's research."

"So, the author has a PI ticket? You can find all sorts of things in cereal boxes these days."

"It's a free country, Rixon. Do you know the identity of the victim in the horse arm case?"

"No. But if I did, I wouldn't tell you. But I'd bet you're going to tell me."

"Do you recognise the name Daniel Anderson?"

The waitress arrived and placed a glass of coke on the table. CS paid for it. Rixon took a swig. 'In the Air Tonight' by Phil Collins had replaced 'Voodoo Child.'

Rixon leaned across the small round table and sneered, "Listen up, Stone, FBI agents ask the questions, not you. Got it?" He rose from his chair.

"Then maybe you should have offered to buy me the drink."

"Very funny. We're done here, Stone. Thanks for the coke."

CS locked eyes with Rixon. "You see, I think Daniel Anderson worked for the NIS and possibly for you or the CIA... perhaps a double agent, and I suspect he was murdered. I intend to prove it one way or another."

Still standing, Rixon lit a cigarette. CS knew he had captured his attention; otherwise, he would have departed. The act of standing up and appearing ready to leave was a tactic.

"One way or another might just get you killed, Stone. This isn't one of your hard-boiled detective novels. The arm didn't belong to Anderson. If you keep searching for its owner, you'll make yourself an even bigger target."

With that said, he began to walk away.

CS called out, "What about Ajeeb Bashir at Dumbo Removals and the Libyans?"

That stopped Rixon in his tracks. He returned to the table, resting his fists on it, glowering at CS, and then growled, "You must be suicidal, buddy. You have no idea what you're meddling with here."

Unperturbed by his theatrics, CS reclined in his chair, tapped a cigarette on his thumbnail, lit it, exhaled a plume of smoke into the air, and stared at Rixon looming over him like a vulture on a branch.

"So, indulge me," CS challenged.

Revealing his irritation like a crimson flag, Rixon pulled out the chair and resumed his seat. He leaned forward once more, and in a conspiratorial tone, he said, "Listen carefully, Stone; all your prying is only serving their purpose—the bad guys. They're tailing your every move. Haven't you noticed? The motorcycle incident, for example?"

"You'd make things much easier if you shared their identities," CS urged.

"That's what we're trying to determine. Look, besides us, the CIA, SIS, and MI6 are involved; it's a joint international effort that we believe could have catastrophic consequences if we fail to shut it down real soon."

"Surely I can assist? If they're tailing me, I'm the perfect bait to draw them out," he echoed Rixon's approach and leaned forward discreetly. "They attacked a friend of mine today; he's in ICU fighting for his life right now. I have a vested interest."

"Colonel Witten. Yes."

CS pulled back, surprised that Rixon was aware. "So, you've got someone tailing me as well?"

"We're tailing your tail," he reiterated as he rose to leave but decided to have the last word. "Look, we need to let this play out to reach the source... we just need to minimize the collateral damage along the way. Watch your back, Stone."

CS sat and pondered until Phil Collins finished his song, then downed his drink and departed.

He navigated through the crowd outside and stopped to hail a taxi. One pulled up but was quickly occupied. Thinking he might have better luck catching one on 6th Avenue, he started up Minetta Lane, a branch off MacDougall Street. The narrow, dimly lit lane wound between six-storey, aging tenement buildings. Car headlights flickered in the lane behind him. He turned sharply, realising he had made a mistake by venturing through a deserted lane after the warning from Rixon. The headlights went dark, but the car ominously continued to follow him. He quickened his pace.

Up ahead, a solitary light almost blinded him. It belonged to a motorcycle that had come to a stop—he was caught between the two vehicles. He glanced quickly at a sign to his left: Minetta Lane Theatre – Currently playing, Blues in the Night. He entered, paid at the box office, and proceeded inside.

The theatre was packed. A jazz quartet graced the stage, with Louis Armstrong at the forefront, singing 'I'm Just A Lucky So and So.' CS slipped into the shadows, waiting to see if he had indeed been tailed. As the song concluded, the audience rose for a standing ovation. A man entered and scanned the area, clearly searching for CS. When he drew closer, CS made his way backstage. Armstrong and the band launched into an encore as CS navigated past crew members and props to reach the loading bay doors and then slipped outside.

In the shadows of the lane, with his back against the wall, CS peeked around the corner of the theatre's entrance. Two men were standing there, smoking, evidently waiting for him. The car that had been trailing him was parked nearby. CS moved stealthily in the opposite direction of the vehicle, heading toward 6th Avenue.

A headlight flared, momentarily blinding him. It was the motorcycle. He came to a halt, shielding his eyes, as it approached. Suddenly, he was grabbed from behind and struck forcefully. Two assailants dragged him into a waiting car.

Another car's headlights illuminated the entrance to the lane leading back to Café Wha!. It had been waiting there.

Inside the car, seated in the front passenger seat, Rixon ordered the driver, "Go!"

The tyres screeched, and the federal agents raced up the lane in pursuit of the car that had taken CS.

First, the motorcycle sped out of Minetta Lane, followed by the car onto 6th Avenue, trailed closely by the federal agents.

Weaving through traffic, the car made a screeching left turn onto West 11th Street just as the traffic lights turned red, thwarting the federal agents.

Frustrated, Rixon slammed both hands on the dashboard. "Damn!"

~ ~ ~

With the Thompson Twins' "Hold Me Now" blaring from the radio in the office, Denise, barefoot, stood on the couch while hanging a picture of CS, herself, and baby Axis in her arms on the office wall. She hopped down, admired her handiwork, and feeling content, grabbed a mop to dance with it to the chorus of the song. The music was so loud that she didn't hear someone knocking at the door. Eventually, the knocking broke through the music, and she turned off the radio before answering the door, hiding the mop behind her back.

Rixon stared at her bare feet and raised an eyebrow. "Mrs Stone?"

Tucking away a loose strand of hair, still slightly out of breath from her dancing, Denise gathered herself and responded, "Yes, and who are you?"

Rixon displayed his badge. "Agent Rixon, ma'am, and this is Agent James. May we come in?"

Denise stepped aside and put away the mop. "Please, have a seat." They complied, and she pulled up a chair opposite them. She suddenly realised she was still barefoot and crossed one foot over the other. The family photo on the wall creaked and tilted slightly. Rixon turned his head to look at it.

"He's putting himself and his family," he glanced back at Denise, "at risk."

Denise felt embarrassed. "I know, I know. What can I say? Once he gets a bug in his bonnet..."

"Tonight, we witnessed his abduction but were unable to prevent it," he stated with a cold tone.

"What?" Denise exclaimed, mortified.

~ ~ ~

I stared at that very photograph still hanging on the wall above the couch and straightened it.

Kendy emerged from her office, took a seat on the couch, and asked, "What's going on?"

"I'm not sure if I can handle what's coming next; it must be close to when Dad gets it."

"After what we've learned, I think you need to talk to Rixon again. We can't ignore the core issue here: were your parents like murdered? If so, by whom and why?"

Her determination helped me regain my composure. "Yeah, you're right." I grabbed my cellphone and dialled. "Rixon... Axis Stone, we need to talk. Yes, I have the disk; I'll trade it for some information. Okay, where and when... not the same place. Good."

"Where this time?" Kendy asked.

"Starbucks, up on Canal Street. It's a five-minute walk."

"Want me along?"

"Absolutely."

After we passed through the Chinese-style façade, Kendy went to order while I grabbed a table. Rixon entered alone. The look on his rugged face suggested that misery was a DIY project for him.

"Agent Rixon, want anything?"

"I'll take a small vanilla latte."

I signalled Kendy at the counter to get one more, and she nodded.

"I hope this isn't another waste of time, Stone," Rixon remarked with an arrogant sneer.

"Oh, I don't think so."

"You obviously found the disk."

"Yes, and someone held a knife to my assistant's throat and took it."

He glanced at the ceiling and quipped, "I'm not surprised."

"I thought it might have been you."

"Not my style. Look, I warned you and your stubborn father to drop it; look where it got him."

Kendy arrived with three coffees just in time, preventing me from taking a swing at the conceited bastard. "This is my assistant, Kendy," I snarled.

"Hello, Agent Rixon," Kendy greeted politely.

Rixon nodded.

"We've reached the point where you failed to stop my Dad from being abducted."

Rixon sighed deeply, his expression disconsolate. "So the disk contains what, a manuscript?... a diary?"

"You could call it that," I said in monotone.

He thought about it a moment, I figured to gather his memory. "Alright, that was the first time I met your mother—quite a smart lady, wasn't she?"

Kendy chuckled, "She was dancing with a mop when you turned up."

His weathered face creased into a wry smile. "Ah, so that's why she had the mop in her hand."

"So, the deal still stands... I'll give you the file if you tell me the name of the horse arm victim."

"Look, I'd love to have that file; it would fill in a few blanks for me. But the truth is, it don't matter no more. It's done... finito, over. Capiche?"

"No, it isn't," I growled. "Who was it?"

"We still don't know. It's classified. If you keep searching, you might eventually find out why. As for who took the disk and who killed Liz Parks—that's for the cops to find out."

"What about the fact that my parents were murdered?"

"There's no evidence to support that."

"Daniel Anderson, who was he?" Kendy asked.

"Never heard of him."

"Yes, you have; my father told you his name in Café Wha!"

"Don't remember," he shrugged his shoulders. "That was long time ago."

He looked visibly unsettled.

"What about the Libyan connection?" I prompted.

"The CIA, SIS, MI6, and the NIS?" Kendy added.

"Yeah. So? Look-it, if you want to give me the file, fine. I can get a court order to obtain it from you if I want, but I don't wanna to do that. Let's keep it within the family," he threw his arms open Italian style." You can run things past me, and I'll tell you what I can. Okay? That's about the best I can do."

"Alright, once we finish reading it, I'll give it to you. Who abducted my Dad that night in Minetta Lane?"

He folded his arms in front of him defensively and said all too quickly for my liking, "We never found out."

His flashing eyes and defensive body language indicated to me he was lying.

I gazed past him, lost in vague contemplation, my eyes fixed on the bustling Centre Street outside.

"What happened after you spoke to Denise?" Kendy inquired.

"I put a tail on her. To keep her safe. It wasn't easy; she was even more crafty than her old man. It was my guy Vernon James... he was waiting outside the Regis Building for her. We knew she had no choice but to go to the cops as soon as we left. James tailed her all the way to the 1st Precinct at NYPD and then must've waited for her while she met with Detective Blake. Vernon was found a block from the NYPD, dead."

"Murdered?" I asked.

"Yeah, injected with a nerve agent."

"That's what you were told killed your parents," Kendy noted.

"Yeah, and it's too much of a coincidence. Who killed Vernon James?" I asked.

"Whoever was tailing Denise. There were a few suspects, but none ever panned out."

"I can't believe how much gets left unsolved with you lot," I snarled.

"Well, it did then. You've gotta remember these were Cold War days; New York was infested with spies because of all the UN activity. By then, every member country had a presence here. No internet, no cellphones… in a lot of ways things in our game were tougher than they are today."

Kendy didn't buy it. "I get that, but you'd think you would've solved cold cases like this by now."

Rixon got up to leave. "If you wanna to know more, talk to Blake; he's probably still around."

"It's obvious the tail who killed James was involved with the abduction of my dad and maybe the visitor after Liz Parks. You'd have to think they still have a rat up their arse; otherwise, they wouldn't have bumped her off. What, after thirty-plus years, they still have something to hide? So what the hell is it?"

"You'll find out; I'm not at liberty to say."

I snapped, "Damn, man! At least tell me who your main suspects were?"

Standing, eyeballing me, he rattled off, "The NIS, the CIA, SIS, MI6, Iran, and the Libyans... take your friggin' pick. Oh, and you can't exclude the KGB; they were still active until 1991 when they became the FSB." With that, he turned and left.

Kendy propped up her chin with her fists, her elbows resting on the table. "His attitude like sucks."

"Tell me about it. He's about as useful as an inflatable dartboard. The only thing truthful he said was that it would've been tough in our game back then."

We sat in contemplative silence for a moment.

"Before we read any more of the manuscript, we need to get Joe Blake's version of the story," I said, dialling Blake's number.

CHAPTER
ELEVEN

It was dusk, and we were gathered around a table in the conference room of the 1st Precinct. Present were Bulldog, Joe Blake, Kendy, and myself.

"So you're now completely up to speed with what we know. I understand the Liz Parks murder is an ongoing case, so I don't expect much from you, Bulldog, but I'd like to hear Detective Blake's take on what happened after my mother came to see him at the NYPD that night."

"Alright, as you know, the horse arm case had been sequestered by the FBI, presumably due to diplomatic implications... I was waiting at the elevator for Mrs Stone. I had met her on several previous occasions: once at my office here and then at the Hatsuhana Sushi Restaurant, both times in connection to the horse arm case. But this time was different; Mrs Stone was claiming her husband had been abducted.

We sat down. She was wringing her hands as she explained the situation. When she mentioned the attack on Colonel Witten and how it was related to Carter's abduction, I decided we should pay the Colonel a visit.

He was sitting up in the hospital bed with his head bandaged over one eye. His secretary, um...."

"Dorris," Kendy prompted.

"Yes, Dorris, it was a while back... was in a bedside chair with a white plaster across her nose. The Colonel was still a bit groggy, but when he was told Carter had been kidnapped, he perked up somewhat. I asked him for a description of his assailant, but he couldn't help; it had all happened too quickly for him. I asked if they'd robbed him. He said they'd only taken the personal file on Daniel Anderson. I had no idea what Anderson had to do with anything, but Dorris piped up and said Carter suspected it was Anderson's arm in the horse arm case. Then Denise asked Dorris if she remembered anything at all about her assailants, and she said she had, that one of them had a New Zealand or South African accent, he'd said, 'Yes, to Dumbo'... she'd remembered because her dad had gotten the movie Dumbo on Betamax... Dumbo, the Flying Elephant. Well, that fired up Denise; she'd realised they must have been talking about Dumbo Removals in Brooklyn."

I said, "Yes, the name was on the side of the truck involved in the Liz Parks hit and run."

"That's right," Blake said, "there was something about photos taken by witnesses of of that incident."

"Yes, a couple from Kentucky took them... CS told them to take them to you at the precinct," Kendy said.

"I never got to see them; they never showed," Blake said.

"The photos motivated CS and Denise to like visit Dumbo Removals, where they encountered a shady character, the manager named Ajeeb Bashir. His niece at the front desk had accidentally dropped that the Libyan Consulate had like rented the truck the hit and run bike had escaped in," Kendy explained.

Blake continued, "Ah, that makes sense... So, with Dorris mentioning Dumbo, I decided to pay the place a visit... I couldn't talk Denise out of coming.

"I was driving... we passed through the Dumbo Archway; I remember there was a lot of chatter that night on the police radio, not uncommon on a full moon.

"I shouldn't be bringing you along; this is likely to be dangerous," I told Denise beside me.

"Don't worry about me, Joe, I can handle myself," she chuckled.

"I'm sure you can, lady."

"What gets me is why Rixon and his Feds aren't involved?" she said.

"I've dealt with them plenty of times; they're a law unto themselves, they don't tolerate interference."

I pulled up a distance from Dumbo Removals and from inside the car, we cased the joint. I noticed a light flash on a window pane in the workshop at the rear.

"See that? A torchlight."

"Yes, yes, there! In the workshop," Denise confirmed.

"Right, now listen to me, you stay in the car while I go check it out. Okay?"

I opened my door to get out, and Denise got out as well.

"What did I just say, damn it!"

"Can't you see I'm ignoring you?" she said in a harsh whisper.

"I drew my gun and cursed just loud enough for her to hear, 'Women!'"

I led Denise into the shadows across the forecourt to the side driveway of Dumbo. If it wasn't for the torchlight we'd seen, you would've thought the joint was vacant... It was close to midnight... we reached the workshop. I tried the door, it was locked. Beside it was the loading bay, with two industrial-size roller doors. A servo sounded. We dived for cover.

The nearest roller door opened. I had my gun aimed at it. We heard voices. Two men ducked under the door while it's rising and walked towards us talking. I stepped out, gun up, and ordered, "NYPD, get your hands up. Now!"

They complied. Then a 3rd man came out of the workshop. He saw me holding the other two up and quickly pulled a gun.

Soon as he saw Denise he swung his aim at her and yelled, "Drop it or she's dead!"

It was a Mexican standoff. In a flash, Denise pulled a gun; I didn't know she was carrying, and fired at the 3rd man. She hit him in the chest, and he went down.

"On the ground now, flat out!" I yelled at the two I had. They hit the deck.

An engine started inside the workshop, and a bright pair of headlights flashed on. Before we had time to move, a car came hurtling out towards us. I dived out of the way. My two prisoners rolled on the ground out of the way, then bounced up and drew their guns.

Denise opened fire at one of them and missed. He aimed at her. I got to my feet. The other guy aimed at me. The car sped off. It looked real bad. Then two shots sounded out of nowhere, and both men went down.

Two men in black stepped out of the darkness with guns up and declared they were CIA agents Robinson and Walker. They told us to hold our fire.

One of the guys hit was dead, and the other one still alive, just but we needed to get him to a hospital, real quick. Denise checked the 3rd guy on the ground and declared that he was in need of a body-bag."

"On our way to the hospital, I inquired of Denise about the source of the gun. She replied that it was the firearm CS had discovered in Anderson's apartment, the one he had presented me the serial number of at the Hatsuhana Sushi Restaurant. We assumed the two CIA agents had been tailing us. It was fortunate they had, or we would've been in serious trouble.

"Outside the ER, Robinson and Walker joined us. It was time to pose some questions.

But before I could utter a word, Robinson stated, "We'll take it from here, Blake."

Denise didn't appreciate that and retorted, "Like hell you will. The guy in surgery knows where my abducted husband is!"

"We're aware of the situation, ma'am," Walker said, "but there's nothing you can do. Go home."

I could see she was on the verge of exploding, so I gently gripped her elbow to silence her. She understood the message. I expressed gratitude to the agents and escorted Denise up the corridor.

Once we were out of earshot of the agents, she growled, "What on earth are you doing?"

I waved a wallet in front of her face and reassured her, "I've got our friend's wallet and gun... with these, we'll be able to trace CS. Don't worry."

Bulldog, Kendy, and I were captivated by Blake's firsthand account.

He continued, "There was nothing we could do, so I dropped Denise off at home. By the next morning, I had received print results from AFIS and the gun registry. It was an unregistered firearm, a burner, we called them then, later that became the term for an anonymous cellphone... The prints had no matches. Our only hope lay in the contents of the wallet. As I was going through it, the chief called and ordered me off the case."

"Could've smelt that one coming once the CIA got involved," Bulldog remarked.

"Yeah, I had a feeling it might happen. What transpired afterward is still off the record... I called Denise and delivered the bad news, then arranged to meet at her office. Later, I was seated on the couch with a coffee in hand.

"There's definitely something peculiar going on. The perp in the hospital is Libyan, and he isn't going to make it. Of the other two, one was Iranian, and the one you shot was South African."

"A regular league of nations. What's your take on that?" Denise inquired.

"With the CIA and the FBI all over it like a cheap suit, there can only be one explanation: a spy ring. That's obviously why I've been taken off the case."

"Any leads from the wallet?"

"Yeah. He might be Libyan, but his address is in New Jersey. I thought we might pay the place a visit."

Denise offered a smug smile. "Thought you were off the case?"

A few hours later, I halted the car at the grand front gates of Ventura Park Stables in New Jersey. The surrounding landscape was lush. On the opposite side of the imposing front gate, a lengthy red pebble driveway led to an elegant two-storey residence, a barn, and stables. White fences, meticulously maintained gardens, horses grazing in fields, and a sign on the gates forbidding unauthorised entry.

"What's your plan?" Denise inquired.

"When in doubt, flash the shield."

I pulled up to the gates, rolled down the window, and displayed my badge to the security camera. Like magic, the gates swung open.

We proceeded up to the house, where we were welcomed by two armed sentinels clad in black military attire.

Denise looked puzzled. "Armed guards for a horse breeding facility? Seems a bit excessive, don't you think?"

We exited the car and approached one of the guards. Before either of us could speak, they conducted a pat-down search. The guard relieved Denise of her gun, but I had no intention of parting with mine.

"I'm with the NYPD. I won't surrender my weapon," I declared.

The guard muttered into his headset in a foreign language, apparently receiving approval, and then escorted us through the imposing front doors.

Inside, we were greeted by a young woman in traditional Middle-Eastern attire, her attractive face unveiled.

"Welcome. My name is Lelia. Mr Rashidi is expecting you in the study," she said with a distinct accent. "Please follow me."

We followed her through the grand house, down a corridor, and then through double doors into a spacious room designed like an English Manor House study: wood panelling, a wall lined with antique books, a substantial antique desk, and a seating area by a large fireplace ablaze with a roaring fire.

Standing with his back to us by the mantelpiece, gazing into the fire, was a tall man with greying hair, impeccably dressed in a fine tailored suit. Lelia motioned for us to take a seat on the couch. The man turned to face us. He was handsome, six feet tall, in his late 40s, and I surmised he was likely of Iranian origin.

He spoke with a refined British accent, "Greetings, Mrs Stone and Detective Blake. My name is Farzin Rashidi. Please have a seat."

We complied, and Leila found a seat as well. Remaining standing with his back to the fireplace, Rashidi continued, "I see you weren't expecting a warm reception."

"On the contrary, I assure you," I responded. "Where is my husband, Mr Rashidi?"

He moved to an armchair, seated himself, and, crossing his long legs, reached for a gold box on a side table. He opened it and offered it to me.

"A cigarette, Detective?"

"This is an official visit, Mr Rashidi," I stated firmly.

"Oh, I doubt that, Detective Blake. Firstly, we are in New Jersey, well beyond your jurisdiction, and secondly, this is a diplomatic matter—a forbidden domain for the NYPD."

"That may be the case, but my department has authorised this inquiry. I do believe Mrs Stone asked you a question."

There was a pregnant pause, and then he said, "Indeed she did. Mrs Stone, your husband will be released on the condition that you agree to immediately cease your true-crime novel writing and terminate all investigations related to the horse arm case. You will sign a waiver to that effect."

Rashidi pressed a button on the side table, and an older woman, resembling a Gestapo officer, entered clutching a document.

CHAPTER TWELVE

I observed the woman in her sixties place the agreement on the coffee table between Denise and Leila. With his gaze fixed on us, Rashidi said, "Give Mrs Stone a pen, Mina."

Scowling, Mina handed Denise a golden pen. She accepted it but avoided eye contact with her, engrossed in reviewing the document. Mina stood by, resembling a vulture perched on a tree branch.

"You can see that your husband has signed the waiver," Rashidi said with an air of arrogance.

"Coercion, no doubt," Denise retorted.

"No, no, not at all, merely persuasion."

"Mr Stone was abducted," I said angrily.

"To the contrary, Detective Blake, he came here of his own volition."

Denise looked up at Rashidi with narrowed eyes. "And I suppose Colonel Witten and his secretary assaulted themselves."

"This is the first I've heard of that. I assure you we were not involved," Rashidi said defensively.

Denise fidgeted with the pen nervously. "And if I refuse to sign?"

"That would not be in the best interests of your family."

Denise placed the agreement and the pen on the table, then reclined in her chair with her arms folded defiantly. "I won't do anything until I see my husband."

Rashidi shot her a wry smirk, then nodded to Mina. She turned and left the room.

I interjected, "Why are you so insistent on having the agreement signed?"

"Let's just say there are sensitive matters at stake here that could be jeopardised if certain information were made public."

"Wouldn't it be better to collaborate with the authorities rather than resorting to all this secrecy?"

Rashidi intertwined his fingers in front of him. "I'm afraid we've already crossed that threshold, Detective."

The door opened, and Mina entered, escorting CS, flanked by two guards. He didn't appear dishevelled as I had expected.

Mina directed the guards to release him, then motioned for him to sit in a chair. Before doing so, CS enveloped Denise in a heartfelt hug.

Tears welled up in Denise's eyes as she asked, "I've been so worried about you, darling. Are you hurt?"

"No, no, I'm fine."

"Please, take a seat, Mr Stone," Rashidi ordered.

CS let go of Denise, nodded at me, and took a seat. I offered him a cigarette, which he accepted, and I provided him with a light.

"Mr Rashidi is insisting I sign this agreement, darling. You've signed it; did you do so willingly?"

"No, I was coerced."

Denise glared at Rashidi and scoffed, "As I suspected."

Rashidi maintained his posture, fingers intertwined in front of him, and calmly stated, "The point is, given your circumstances, you are obligated to sign."

Denise glanced sharply at CS. "What should I do, Carter? It was your decision to pursue this case."

I inquired, "What happens once she signs?"

Rashidi unfolded his fingers and spread his arms in a pious manner. "The three of you will be free to leave."

Leila signalled to Mina to hand Denise back the contract and pen. Denise hesitated to take them, awaiting CS's approval. CS glared at

Rashidi, then at his wife, and nodded. Denise retrieved the contract and pen from Mina, signed it, and declared, "I want a copy of the executed agreement."

"Mina, please make a photocopy of it," Rashidi ordered.

Mina took back the pen and the document and then departed.

Leila spoke up, "I apologise for not being the most accommodating host; I should have offered you—"

Denise brazenly interrupted her, "Thanks, but the poison-pen was an ample paragon of your purpose."

CS and I stood to leave. Denise sprang up and strode assertively toward the door, where Mina was waiting with the photocopy. Denise snatched it irreverently from her grasp.

~ ~ ~

Stretching an elastic band between his fingers, Blake took his seat at the table. "On the way back to Manhattan, CS briefed us on the abduction."

"I suppose that explains why the book was never published. But it didn't end there, did it?" I asked Blake.

"Did for me. Got me discharged, had to move to Albany and start over again with the NYSP."

Kendy appeared lost in thought and then asked, "So... What's next?"

I rose from my seat. "We have a case to solve, that's what."

Bulldog stood up and locked eyes with me. "Just shout if you need me."

Blake also stood and extended his hand for a handshake. "Good luck, Axis."

~ ~ ~

A while later, I found myself pacing the office floor, wearing out the carpet. Kendy was on the couch, watching me closely.

"Nothing ties it all together," I grumbled.

"I know, it's baffling. So, this Rashidi guy pressures your parents into like signing the waiver. Blake is taken off the case, again..."

Kendy was interrupted by a knock at the door.

"Who could that be at this hour? I'll get it," I said. I opened the door to find Linus and Booker. "Hey, fellers! Come on in."

As they entered, Linus, leaning on a walking stick, spoke up, "Thought it was about time we checked in for an update. Hello, Kendy. This is my cousin, Booker."

Kendy made room on the couch for them.

"What's with the walking stick, Linus?" I inquired.

"You know you've reached a certain age when you forget that you've forgotten something," Linus cryptically replied.

The three of us shared a chuckle, and I pressed, "What's that mean?"

Sitting on the couch, Linus searched his inside jacket pocket for something. "Well, I knew there was something I needed to give you, but I kept forgetting to remember it." He produced an envelope and handed it to me. "Your mother entrusted this to me for safekeeping."

"And here," Booker added, producing an envelope of his own. "I managed to get this."

"Christmas cards already?" I teased.

I opened Linus's envelope first, read it, and then passed it to Kendy.

Kendy looked up from reading it. "It's a photocopy of the contract with Rashidi."

I opened Booker's envelope. "Hmm, the toxicology reports from pathology."

"You'll see they match; Ricin, which can cause death through multiple organ failure or cardiovascular shock."

Kendy examined the reports. "So these were like ignored?"

"Too late, I was told. The examiner had already submitted his report. I sent copies of these to many influential people, but nothing was done," Booker said, his expression solemn. "It was a massive cover-up."

"Thank you, my friends," I said, trying to lift our spirits. "Come on, I'll walk you downstairs; it's time to call it a day."

I inserted my key into the lock of my apartment door, but it creaked open as I turned it. Cautiously, I drew my gun, assumed a stealthy stance, and gently pushed the door open further with my foot. With my gun at the ready, I slipped inside and paused to scan the room. A tall, imposing figure stood silhouetted in front of the window, holding a firearm behind his back.

I immediately commanded, "Drop the gun and turn around slowly."

He complied, but instead of dropping the weapon, he retained his grip on it. I snapped my fingers, and the corner lamp illuminated the room.

"I remember that trick," he grumbled.

"Well, well, look who's paid a visit, none other than Handerson Bolt, the hitman. Is this some sort of personal vendetta?" I inquired.

"Not quite, Stone... It's a new job. Imagine my delight when I found out the target was you."

"I've never noticed your South African accent before."

"How observant of you."

"So, is the job to eliminate me?"

"Not yet. This is just a warning shot across the bow," he replied with a sneer.

"A warning of what?" I challenged.

"Drop the case."

"Who's giving the orders?"

"Al Head's superior." He lowered his gun and walked confidently toward me. I held my ground. He bumped me forcefully as he passed, shoulder to shoulder, and then headed for the exit. With my back to the door, I holstered my gun. Suddenly, Bolt swung around sharply and pistol-whipped me from behind. I went down, dazed but not defeated, and looked up at Bolt, who stood over me.

"For the time you locked me in the trunk," he snarled.

~ ~ ~

The following day, I found Kendy already hard at work when I arrived at the office.

She greeted me with concern, "You look a bit rough."

"I had an unwelcome visitor last night who introduced me to the business end of his gun."

She got up to examine my head, "Sit down, let me take a look." I sat in her chair, and she carefully inspected my scalp.

"Ew, that's quite a bump… you must have a serious headache."

"It feels more like a marching band."

"Who attacked you?"

"An old adversary… Handerson Bolt, the hitman."

Kendy recoiled, "The same guy I read about in the opal case report. The guy you like left locked in the trunk of a car at San Francisco airport?"

"That's him. And the fact that he's South African seems like too much of a coincidence."

"Do you think it's connected to our current case?"

"Highly likely. He warned me to drop it."

"Why do these criminals always have to make things so complicated?"

"It comes with the turf."

"Oh, before I forget, there was a somewhat sketchy cryptic message on the answering machine."

"Sketchy cryptic?"

"Man, I think it's time we invested in a new machine; like the old one is seriously past its use-by-date."

"Sure, who left the message?"

"Richard Harris. He found an ancient artefact but someone stole it. Needs a private investigator to get it back."

"Sounds interesting, but for now, it'll have to go on our bucket list."

Kendy was at her desk and opened the file on her laptop. "We can fast forward until after they leave the ranch."

"Okay, I'll just pick up after that... the next day...

~ ~ ~

Denise was preparing Axis for day-care when the phone rang. CS called out from the bathroom of the Manhattan apartment.

"I'll get it!"

He rushed from the bathroom into the living room bare-chested with his face covered in shaving cream, much to the amusement of Axis, who erupted with hysterical laughter.

"Hello. How are you? Good to hear. You have? Okay, we'll call past on our way to the office. Thank you."

Denise arrived, holding young four-year-old Axis in her arms, who was still giggling at his father. "Who was it, love?" She asked.

"The Colonel. He wants us to call by to show us something."

She pulled a quizzical face. "But aren't we off the case?"

"Yes, yes, I know... but—"

He was interrupted by the door buzzer.

"That'll be Sofia." She pressed the intercom. "Hello."

A small Filipino-accented voice replied, "It's just Sofia, Mrs Stone."

CS playfully put a dab of shaving cream from his face on Axis' nose. They both giggled. He headed back to the bathroom to shave.

"I'll bring him down, Sofia." She replied then called out to CS, "You nearly ready, hon?"

CS called back, "Yep, meet you downstairs."

Denise told Axis, "Say bye-bye to Daddy."

Axis called out, "Bye-bye, Dadda!"

CS charged back out of the bathroom, wiping his face with a towel and kissed his cute little fair-haired boy. "See ya, little general."

They saluted one another like soldiers, and then Denise carried the lad out through the door.

~ ~ ~

It had me welling up. I said, "That was the last time I saw my dad."

Kendy turned from the laptop and said sympathetically, "Oh, that must be like such a painful memory for you."

"Funny, that's not exactly how I recall that day. Ha! Little general, I'd forgotten he used to call me that." After a sigh, I said, "Okay, let's continue."

"You sure you're alright?"

"Yep," I lied. "So... Next stop was the Golden Dawn in Hell's Kitchen."

~ ~ ~

Denise and CS were seated opposite the Colonel in his office at the Golden Dawn. Dorris entered carrying a tray of coffees, still with a white plaster across the bridge of her nose. She was also grasping a folder under her arm.

She placed the tray on the coffee table then handed Colonel Witten the folder. "Anything else?" she inquired.

"That'll be all, thanks, Dorris."

She gave CS a wink on the way out, which both Denise and the Colonel caught.

"Don't worry about her dalliances, Denise. She flirts with anyone in pants. So, what happened was after we had that meeting about our friend Anderson, I used our new gadget, a facsimile machine, to send an info request on him to our Stockholm chapter... you might recall, CS, that's where he was nominated. In it, I requested if they had anything more on him because he was missing. I received this reply."

He selected a document from the folder and handed it to CS.

"It says Daniel Anderson is wanted by Interpol for suspected terrorist activity."

"Wow, how did he manage to come here with a charge like that hanging over his head?" Denise said.

"Under an assumed name? That might explain why we haven't been able to trace him; he's probably been using an alias."

The Colonel nodded, "Makes sense."

Denise was dismissive. "It makes no difference anyhow, we're off the case."

"Oh, why is that?" asked the Colonel, surprised.

"It has become a diplomatic hot potato," Denise said facetiously.

"We've been ordered to drop it or we might get our fingers burnt," CS said, ruefully.

That didn't go down too well with the Colonel, and he protested tersely, "Ordered? By whom, pray tell?"

"Farzin Rashidi, the FBI, the CIA, MI6, you name it... all the spooks."

"Who on Earth is Farzin Rashidi?" he snarled.

CS lit up a cigarette while glancing at Denise. "You know, that's a question we've not bothered to ask."

The Colonel was incensed, "This is America, son! There's a thing here called the First Amendment."

He sounded like Foghorn Leghorn.

"Yep, freedom of speech. You're damned right, Colonel," CS thundered, much to the distaste of Denise.

A few minutes later, Denise and CS, arm in arm, were walking the busy pavement. "The Colonel is right, love; they can't shut us down."

"But we signed a contract," she disputed.

"We don't even know who with, for God's sake."

She stopped him. "Alright then, I'll investigate Farzin Rashidi, but remember how dangerous this is. We've been warned, at the first sign of trouble, we're out. Promise?"

"Okay, okay... So, now we know Anderson used an alias. If we can find out what it is, it will go a long way to solving the whole shebang. I think we can do that without attracting any undue attention."

"I hope you're right, Carter Stone. I hope you're right."

~ ~ ~

In her office, looking studious wearing glasses, Denise was on the phone taking notes. CS was in the main office reclined in his chair with his feet up on the desk, also chatting on the phone. They simultaneously ended their calls, both appearing frustrated.

Denise called out to CS, "I've spent half a day ringing around trying to run down information on Farzin Rashidi and drawing a blank. How are you doing?"

"I can't believe this nonsense! Everything draws a blank. Anderson must have been a CIA asset."

Denise wandered up to Carter's desk, sat on the edge of it, and looked jaded, removed her glasses, and tiredly pinched the bridge of her nose.

"The glasses make you look hot," CS said with an amorous glint in his eye.

"That's just your penchant for librarian types," she said, putting the glasses back on and crossing her bare legs while alluringly drawing her skirt up above her knee.

"Penchant! You spoke French!" CS said, mimicking John Austin playing Gomez Addams in the famous 60s television series. Drawn like a moth to a flame, he leapt out of his chair, took her in his arms, and whispered alluringly in her ear, "We're getting nowhere here, let's go home and make love all night."

"Wearing my glasses?" Denise purred sensually.

"Only your glasses," he insisted flirtatiously.

They kissed passionately. It was getting heated when... the phone rang. Still kissing, he reached for it on his desk and answered it, his voice muffled with his lips not leaving hers. "Carter Stone... Hello... hello?" He abruptly pulled out of their embrace, leaving Denise intrigued. The phone rang in Denise's office. She hopped up and went to answer it. After a few moments, Denise returned. "That was Sofie; she can't babysit tonight. We'll have to go home now. Who called you?"

"Believe it or not, old Mrs Goldstein. She was clearing out Anderson's room and found a locked briefcase under the bed."

CS was excited by the possibility of unearthing more clues to Anderson's identity, but Denise was less enthusiastic.

"We'll go in the morning."

"We can't; she wants us to collect it now."

"Never rains; it pours. Okay, we'll take a cab and swing past. You can duck in and grab it," she said reticently.

CHAPTER THIRTEEN

The taxi pulled up outside the 29th Avenue apartment block. CS stepped out onto the pavement, holding the rear door open, and said to Denise in the back seat, "Okay, give me five." He leaned in and gave her a peck on the cheek.

Denise watched him go up to the front door, press the intercom, and then enter.

A few moments later, the door to the entrance opened, and a man in a dark suit carrying a briefcase exited and walked up the street. It was a false alarm. Denise looked at her watch. The cab's metre and the engine were running; the driver looked impatient. She murmured to herself, "Damn it, CS, where are you?"

Up ahead of the cab, a parking cop was making his way towards them. The driver looked up at Denise in the rear-view mirror.

"Parking cop's coming, lady, I gotta move."

Denise looked up sharply as the entrance door opened again. This time it was Mrs Goldstein, and she was waving her walking stick to attract Denise's attention.

"I need to go inside the apartments, can you wait?" she almost pleaded with the driver.

"No, lady, I'll get booked."

"Alright, alright, here." She paid him, got out, and then met Mrs Goldstein at the door.

In a terrible flap, the old lady said, stuttering, "I, I didn't know what to do...!" She headed off into the dark corridor, followed by Denise. "I let him into 202, then I went back to my room," she said, puffing out of breath as they negotiated the staircase faster than Denise had expected her to do. "Then, I heard a loud noise." They reached the open door of apartment 202 and went in. "I found him on the floor."

A sudden panic came over Denise, as she entered the bedroom. CS was on the floor out cold. She knelt down beside him and felt for a pulse; to her horror, she couldn't find it. She cried out to Mrs Goldstein standing in the doorway. "Quick, call an ambulance!"

Denise scanned the room for the briefcase, stood up, and then checked under the bed and in the wardrobe. She combed the room for it and found nothing. Giving up, she sat back down on the floor and rested her husband's head in her lap. She took his hand. His fist was clenched. She unfurled his fingers. In his hand was a note. She pocketed it, then noticed his lips had turned blue. She quickly opened one of his eyelids, and the eye was rolled back. He wasn't breathing. She immediately gave him CPR.

Mrs Goldstein appeared back in the doorway and said, "The ambulance will be five minutes, is he—?"

Denise had tears streaming down her cheeks as she desperately administered CPR. "I don't know, I think I'm losing him... where's the briefcase?"

"I, I don't know... I, I, I gave it to him."

"Was there someone else here?"

She thought for a moment, "You know... I did hear something."

Later, a crowd of onlookers had besieged the ambulance on the sidewalk in front of the apartment block with its lights flashing. From out of the apartments came two paramedics wheeling a gurney with CS on it. Denise was beside it, her face pale, holding CS's hand. She let it go for him to be loaded into the rear of the ambulance. Mrs Goldstein watched on while chatting animatedly with neighbours. Denise shot Mrs Goldstein a sad wave, and she climbed into the ambulance to accompany her husband to the hospital. The ambulance sped off, siren blazing.

~ ~ ~

On a bench outside the ER, Denise had her head cradled in her hands. She was waiting alone, anxious, her leg nervously bouncing up and down. A surgeon in a green gown and mask came out through the swinging doors and approached her. She looked up at him with her eyes flooded with fear, pain, and tears. He gently placed a consoling hand on her shoulder. She broke down.

Time passed in fast motion, but not for Denise; she was in slow motion, seated, grappling with the pain of losing her husband. People moved in and out of the corridor. Eventually, she got up and walked mournfully towards the exit at a different pace than the rest of the world—lost and heartbroken.

I was standing, staring at the framed book covers on the wall of Kendy's office, choked up after reading of my father's death. A hand on my shoulder made me flinch; it was Kendy's.

"Hey, wanna like grab some air?"

I faced her with my eyes brimming with tears and nodded affirmatively.

~ ~ ~

It was a cloudy, blustery day. We walked down James Street in silence towards St. James Place, then turned right. We came to St. James Triangle and sat on a park bench. The autumn leaves from the now bare trees were blowing about our feet with each gust of wind.

"That was like pretty tough for you."

I sat back, laced my fingers behind my head, crossed my legs, and sighed, "Yeah, well, I guess I knew it was coming."

"What was it like growing up with folks who virtually lived at the office?"

"Never really noticed it. When we were together, it made up for it. I was a bit of a loner anyway."

"So you were like so young when you lost them. I can't imagine what it would be like."

"They both died within a short time of one another. From then on, I was raised by my Filipina nanny, Sofia. Her kids had grown up, she was written into the will to care for me until I could care for myself. I think even Linus was written in as a guardian."

"Wow, a Filipino governess and a black guardian, you, my man, were brought up multicultural."

"I would have traded anything for the folks to have survived; they must have been an incredible couple, wish I'd known them."

"So why a PI and not an author? You know, like following in those incredible footsteps."

"Shoes were too big to fill. You know, those early years I somehow picked up on investigating from them, must be in my DNA."

"Probably."

"I tried a stack of things, a rock muso, actor but found my feet when I got a PI licence in Aussie."

"No thoughts of like settling down; a family and all?"

"In the last year I've had opportunities to do that but hey, I'm crap to live with, but I'm a good screw."

"Yeah, I get that, I'm much the same. A bad time with a guy landed me my daughter and turned me vagitarian."

"Hey, whatever turns you on."

"Exactly."

The Terrible Tango rang out.

"I love that song," Kendy said with a smile.

I answered. "Hello, Stone. Hey! Carlos, nice to hear your croaky voice. What's up?"

"Thought I'd better let you know—"

"Don't say it…. Handerson Bolt is on the loose. How the hell did he get out?"

"A good attorney. Seems you've already had a visit, huh?" Santana said.

"Yep, with a warning that Al Head's boss has hired him to

convince me to drop the case I'm on."

"Well, now you're here in the Big Apple, I thought I need to warn you to watch your ass."

"Yeah, I hear you, buddy."

"Listen, I spoke to Beleza a couple of days ago… she has legally adopted Samantha. You could do yourself a favour and drop by them."

"When I get this done."

"Okay, be careful, son. You know you can call me if you need."

I put the phone away. "That was the LAPD detective from the opal case."

"Santana, the guy you call Carlos?"

"Yes."

"You know you write up your case reports like a novel; I think you like seriously underestimate your talent."

"Come on," I said dismissively, getting up from the bench. "Let's get back to work; we've got a crime to solve."

We headed back toward the office. Feeling the cold, I said, "I think we're going to need some allies on this case."

"I think our best ally is Denise; I'm sure there are more clues to come."

It started to rain, so we made a run for it.

Back at the office, I continued reading the manuscript, which Denise had obviously written in the third person to conceal her identity as the author because of the contract they'd signed with Rashidi.

"Once she learned CS had died from cardiac arrest, she retreated into an emotional cocoon. It was a call from their good friend Booker a week later that snapped her out of it."

~ ~ ~

Booker was at his desk writing when Denise entered. He immediately jumped to his feet and gave her a big, caring hug.

"I nearly passed out when CS came in. I can't tell you how sorry

I am, Denise."

Teary-eyed, she said with a sniffle, "I'm still numbed by it, Booker. Is he still here?"

"No, no, he went to the parlour two days ago after the medical examiner submitted his official report."

She glanced down at her shoes, conscious of choking up again. "Yes, a heart attack… who would have thought…"

Booker took her hand. "Sit down, honey. What I'm going to tell you, well, it won't be easy. It will shock you, then make you very angry. You'll need to control it, okay?"

With a questioning look on her pretty face, she complied. Still holding her hand, he continued, "Like you, I couldn't believe CS had died from a coronary, so I went against the coroner's findings and did some tests of my own. First, a BNP for heart disease; it was negative. That set alarm bells ringing because the report said it was positive, and that caused me to do more pathology. I sent off a sample to a friend at an independent lab." He let go of her hand and produced a report from the pocket of his lab coat. "Are you sure you're okay with this?"

"Yes," she said wide-eyed as she took the document. "What am I reading here, Booker?"

"A lot of different tests, but there, see what that says?"

"Ricin?"

"Yes, a nerve agent that causes death by multiple organ failure and cardiovascular shock."

Denise stared at her friend, stunned. "Are you saying this nerve agent mimicked a heart attack?"

"I sure am."

"And the medical examiner missed it?"

"Yes. It took until today for me to get the results. When I submitted them, they were ignored."

"Why?"

"Colour?… I'm just an assistant."

Denise reacted angrily, "That's racism. I, I, I'll appeal!"

"Won't help; what you need to do is find out why he was murdered."

Now she was stunned. "Murdered?" she exclaimed.

~ ~ ~

A few days later, after the funeral, in the office, to the sound of Robert Palmer singing 'Simply Irresistible' on the radio, Denise was busy typing on her Macintosh 512. Work was the only way to distract her from her grieving. She had picked up from where her husband had left off: with the slip of paper that had been clutched in his hand. On it was the ten-digit number 2237864538. What does it represent was the conundrum: a passport number? No. A phone number? No.

Dorris was at her desk at the Golden Dawn Society, typing on her Mac, looking more like Cindy Lauper than Cindy Lauper. She looked up sharply at Denise entering.

"Oh, hi Denise. How are you, darling? The ceremony was lovely… nice touch playing Pink Floyd's 'Learning to Fly.'"

"It was one of his favourites. Colonel there?"

"Yep, go right on through."

The Colonel was at his desk. He rose at attention when Denise entered. He hugged her awkwardly and motioned her to sit in the lounge setting. "Are you alright, my dear? I mean, you look lovely… but—"

"Yes, Colonel. Like I told you on the phone, there is reason to suspect foul play with Carter's death. He had this in his hand when I found him. I need to know if it means anything to you?"

She handed him the sliver of paper. He studied it.

"Is it a phone number?"

"No."

"It's not a file or a membership number; they're alphanumeric," he said, handing it back.

"It must be important… he wouldn't have gone to the trouble of scribbling it down in his dying hand."

"Did you notice anything odd that day?"

"Not really, I was in a taxi waiting outside. Wait... yes... there was something. A suspicious-looking man came out of the building and hurried off."

"Describe him."

"Tall, he was in a dark business suit...." The revelation had her on the edge of her seat. "And he was carrying a briefcase... what if it was the briefcase?"

"What briefcase?"

"The one CS was there to collect: Anderson's briefcase. It was murder... and I saw the murderer!"

"There must have been something in that briefcase important enough to commit murder. Perhaps you should look deeper into the Interpol charges against Anderson..."

She thought for a moment then asked, "Any chance you can find out which Interpol office and a contact?"

"I'll get Dorris onto it right away and call you when I have something."

~ ~ ~

A British Airways Concorde touched down at Heathrow Airport, London.

It had been arranged for Denise to meet up with Interpol agent Ann Temple, who had come down from Manchester for the meeting held in a special room at the airport.

Denise was met by a young, attractive officer at the airbridge. It wasn't necessary for her to complete customs or immigration because she was escorted to the special room that existed neither in the UK nor anywhere else. It was called no-man's-land.

Denise entered the room that had a board table with twenty seats around it. Her escort left. Seated at the board table was Ann Temple, a blonde, about the same age as Denise, immaculately dressed in a navy blue business suit. Ann rose to her feet to greet Denise.

"Mrs Stone. Lovely to meet you. My sincere condolences. I'm Ann Temple," she said warmly but business-like and offered her hand to shake.

They sat, and Denise said, "My husband died in pursuit of information on Daniel Anderson."

"Yes, I'm aware of Carter Stone's crime fiction, but are you investigating the subject in an amateur capacity? A personal issue?"

"You could say that. The objective is to uncover the identity of the person who murdered my husband."

"But didn't your husband die of a heart attack?"

"I have good reason to suspect otherwise."

Ann eyeballed her for a moment, evaluating her, and then opened a folder on the table in front of her. "You realise under the circumstances I can only provide you with limited information."

"Yes, I expected that. I'll just ask you questions that you can choose to answer or not."

Ann closed the folder and sat back, ready to take the questions.

"Fine. Proceed."

"Does the number 2237864538 mean anything to you?"

"No."

"What are your charges against Anderson?"

"We believe, in late 1987, he assassinated a Namibian government official named Mutonga Indongo."

"Namibian, interesting. Why?"

"We suspect Anderson of being a National Intelligence Service agent."

"Connected with South African apartheid?"

"The NIS is, yes."

"What does that have to do with Namibia?"

"Okay, a large British mining company, which shall remain nameless, was investigated this year by the UN over a secret deal to import yellowcake from the Rossing Uranium mine in Namibia. The major shareholders in that mine are the governments of South Africa and Iran. You know that South Africa occupies Namibia illegally, yes? The US placed sanctions on Namibia over the deal, which upset Iran, South Africa, and Britain. Indongo was an official leading the way for

Namibia to reclaim independence through the UN."

"So, Daniel Anderson assassinated him?"

"We also believe Anderson is a double agent under an assumed name."

"A double agent with whom?"

"I can't answer that."

"My husband and I have been researching the case of a severed arm that had been sewn inside the torso of a horse that was jagged in the Hudson River in New York. We believe that arm belonged to Daniel Anderson."

"I'm aware of the incident, but without prints, ID cannot be confirmed."

Denise became a little more forceful. "Anderson has been missing since the arm turned up. We made the connection through the Golden Dawn Society in New York. We also got his address. His landlady hadn't seen him in some time, his apartment hadn't been lived in. We found a pistol there with a serial number to a US agency, FBI or CIA. The landlady contacted us when she found a briefcase belonging to Anderson under the bed; my husband was killed when he went to collect it. That suggests the arm was Anderson's, and that somebody doesn't want that known."

"It's no wonder you sell so many crime fiction books, Mrs Stone; that's a compelling story. I think you could well be correct in some of your assumptions."

"Where do Libyans fit into this Namibia thing?"

"Who said anything about Libyans?" Ann asked coolly.

"Have you heard of Farzin Rashidi?"

"Now, there's a name that resonates. He's a significant figure on the Rossing Uranium Mine board of directors."

"Aha. What if Anderson was selling intel to the highest bidder? Seems he had a foot in all doors."

"For your own health, Mrs Stone, I'd let it go if I were you."

The trip to London had been enlightening for Denise, but two conundrums had left her intrigued; the number 2237864538 and the Namibian-Libyan connection.

CHAPTER
FOURTEEN

I reclined in my chair, nimbly flicking a ballpoint between my fingers. Kendy swivelled around to face me.

"You look confused," she said.

"How many pages to go?"

"Only five, it ends abruptly."

"Have you read it?"

"Yes, couldn't help myself. I always read the last page early in mysteries."

"So mum dies on November 9th. I wonder if the date is relevant? And this number 2237864538, is that solved?"

"She doesn't decode it; well, at least she doesn't mention it again. Can't be that important."

"Important enough for it to be the last thing dad ever wrote. Seeing you skipped ahead, what did you find most crucial?"

"I only speed-read it. A few things, but you need to read them in context. I've gotta pick Phoenix up from preschool for a dentist appointment; why don't you finish reading it? I'll be back in an hour or so."

"No sweat."

Kendy left me reading.

~ ~ ~

It was still a blustery day outside, but at least the rain had stopped. Kendy pushed open the front door to Little Ones Preschool. Inside, kids were playing, supervised by their carer. Kendy couldn't spot her daughter, Phoenix, among the children. She was approached by the carer.

"Patricia, hi. I'm here to collect Phoenix for the dentist, but I can't see her…"

"Kendy, yes, we were wondering why Phoenix hadn't come in today."

Struck by panic, Kendy rushed for the door, dialling her cellphone. When it answered, she stopped in the doorway, cursing to herself, "Message bank… damn. Mamma, I'm on my way there to pick up Phoenix, it's like a quarter past one, I'll be five minutes."

~ ~ ~

I was at Kendy's desk, eating a sandwich while reading the manuscript on her laptop when the Terrible Tango played. I answered; it was Kendy in a fluster.

"Kendy, calm down, what's happened?"

"My mother has been assaulted… he took Phoenix, kidnapped her…"

I bounded out of the chair and rushed for the door. "Hush, hush, kid, calm down. Text me the address… I'm on my way."

I was racing along James Street, dodging pedestrians when I got a text alert. I slowed down to a fast walk to read the text. It said, 'You were warned. HB.' I growled, "Bolt, you bastard." I fast-dialled… "Carlos, I need you to call Detective Bixby at NYPD… Bolt just kidnapped my PA's daughter. Okay, thanks mate, yes, Bixby. No, I'll text him the address." I quickly texted the address to Bulldog and then resumed running. It was quicker to have the two cops, Santana and Bulldog talking, so they could mobilise their troops.

~ ~ ~

Kendy was on the lounge with her arm around her mum when the buzzer sounded. She saw me on the screen and pressed enter. She waited nervously at the door. I knocked; she checked through the peephole and then unlatched the door. I came in and took her by the shoulders and looked into her eyes. "I've heard from the kidnapper; it's Handerson Bolt. I've got Santana and Bulldog on the case; we should get a call from them any minute." I walked her over to her mum. "Are you alright, Mrs Lee?" Only a small woman, probably in her early forties, the family resemblance was obvious. She was relatively calm.

"Yes, just a little shaken. I was just leaving with little Phoenix when he snatched her from me then pushed me over. I knocked my head on the wall and blacked out."

The Terrible Tango sounded. I answered, "Carlos, he's on his way, good, much appreciated, my friend. That's great... bring a warm coat."

Seated beside her mother and calmer, Kendy asked, "What did he say?"

"Bulldog's on his way, Santana will fly in tonight."

Sniffling, Kendy asked, "Did you get to read any more of the manuscript?"

"Got to the week after the London trip when Denise gets a call from Eisha, the girl from Dumbo Removals, they're going to meet up."

~ ~ ~

Wearing his glasses, Linus was in his armchair, reading the Villager newspaper. He was distracted by the resonating sound of a child whimpering outside in the lobby. He went back to reading but then heard it again. He struggled up and, assisted by his walking stick, made for the front door all the while mumbling to himself, "Those kids again, playing... I'll scare you off..." he chuckled sinisterly but in jest. He opened the door and, raising his stick with an angry face to frighten them, froze. There was a cute black girl in pigtails sitting on the bottom step of the staircase, sobbing.

Linus slowly lowered his stick and said warmly, "What are you crying for, sweetie?"

The little girl looked up at him with big brown eyes and muttered, "I want my momma."

Linus hobbled over to her and then struggled to sit down beside her on the step. "What's your momma's name, honey?"

"She's Kendy Lee."

"Oh, well, let's see if we can call Kendy Lee, okay?" He pulled his cellphone from the side pocket of his cardigan and dialled.

~ ~ ~

I was standing at the window, looking into the street for Bulldog. He just turned up when the Terrible Tango sounded. I answered.

"Linus, what's up? Yes, she's here... I'll put her on... Kendy, it's Linus."

Kendy got up from the lounge and took the phone from me. "Hello, Linus?" she burst into tears. "Phoenix, darling!" She looked all teary-eyed at her mum, "It's Phoenix on the phone; she's with Linus at the office..." Mrs. Lee was on her feet and emotional. "Is she alright?" "Are you okay, sweetheart?... Yes, mamma, she's all good; Linus is playing games with her... Yes, I'll be there soon, sweetheart. Bye-bye, I love you." She handed me the phone and then hugged her mum. The door buzzer sounded.

"That'll be Bulldog," I told them.

~ ~ ~

A while later, at my office, I was behind my desk with Bulldog seated on the couch.

"This is the second shot across the bows from Handerson Bolt."

"I've put out an APB. Santana sent me all he has on him. A real bad bastard."

"Carlos will be in tonight."

"Why Carlos?" Bulldog asked.

"He prefers it... after his rock namesake Carlos Santana, he even looks like him."

"Funny, I didn't have him pictured like that from his voice."

The door opened, and Kendy came in. Bulldog gave her a little room to sit on the couch; luckily, she was relatively skinny.

"Linus and Phoenix are getting on like a house on fire. She said there was another man with Bolt who was missing a pinky."

"The guy that assaulted you and took the disk. That adds up."

"So Bolt ain't working solo, my guess is we're talking about the mob here," Bulldog said, struggling to get up. "Well, off I go to catch crooks. I'll hook up with Santana in the AM. In the meantime, you better watch your ass, Axis. You want a uniform on your apartment door, Kendy?"

"I think we'll be good with the security from now on, Bulldog."

I got up and opened the door for the big man.

"We need to get this bastard before he gets you. What the hell's the beef anyway?"

"I guess I'm getting too close to the truth. Goddamned stupid of me not to expect this."

"Yeah, buddy, remember, you ain't bulletproof."

I held my hands up in mock surrender, "Got me there, mate, but I can do an excellent impression of God," I joked.

Bulldog almost went cross-eyed, "Sorry, not religious."

I chuckled and closed the door after him. I really liked his wicked sense of humour.

"You wanna go chill with your mum and kid?" I asked Kendy.

"No, I'd sooner finish the manuscript with you. We need to like nail this Handerson Bolt dude."

We went into Kendy's office, and I resumed reading the manuscript.

"She says the rendezvous with Eisha was at the Ear Inn on Spring Street..."

As Denise entered the Ear Inn, she was enveloped in the

pulsating rhythm of INXS's "I Need You Tonight" blaring from the in-house sound system. The establishment was bustling, and she navigated her way to the bar, scanning the crowd until she spotted Eisha. Eisha had transformed from the girl behind the counter at Dumbo Removals; she was now dressed up for a night out with friends. Eisha saw Denise, waved excitedly, and signalled her friends to wait as she made her way through the throng.

Denise had to raise her voice to be heard over the chatter and the music. "Hi Eisha."

"When I read in the papers that your husband had died, I felt sorry for you."

"Thank you…"

"Listen, I can't stay… but I overheard my uncle, here," Eisha said with a sly smile, handing Denise a slip of paper. "Don't look now. I don't know what it means, but it's a closely guarded secret of my uncle's, and I think it's related to what you were asking about."

"Thank you. I'm surprised he lets you come to a place like this."

"He doesn't know!" she said in an emphatic whisper, looking about as though there might be spies in the crowd. "He would kill me if he did! Goodbye. Good luck." She smiled warmly and then skilfully manoeuvred her way back to her friends.

Denise exited the Ear Inn, grateful for Eisha's courageous assistance. The street outside was bustling with activity. She paused to search for a taxi but found none in sight. Determined to increase her chances of finding one, she headed towards Greenwich Street. While walking, she had a nagging suspicion someone was following her. She stole a quick glance over her shoulder and spotted a man in a dark suit who bore a striking resemblance to the individual who had hurried out of the apartment building clutching a briefcase on the day CS had been murdered.

Panic surged through her, and in a desperate attempt to shake off her pursuer, she swiftly crossed Spring Street. To her alarm, the man followed suit. Rain began to pour down, soaking her as she ran. Ahead, she saw a taxi stopping to discharge a passenger. With her tail closing in, Denise sprinted for the taxi. Her high-heeled pumps impeded her progress, so she hopped on one foot, hastily kicked off one shoe, and then repeated the manoeuvre with the other, leaving her barefoot and able to run more swiftly carrying her shoes.

As she reached the taxi, another woman was racing toward it. A quick glance over her shoulder confirmed that her pursuer was closing in. Determined to reach the cab before the other woman, Denise and the stranger arrived at the rear door simultaneously, engaging in a brief struggle for the handle. The menacing figure behind her drew closer. In a moment of desperation, Denise pushed the other woman aside, secured a seat in the cab, and locked the door. The thwarted woman pounded her fists on the window, venting her anger. The pursuer, growing furious, wrested the woman away and attempted to open the front door. Rain pounded on the cab's roof, creating a deafening cacophony.

Denise shouted at the cab driver, "Drive, quickly, get moving!" The cab sped off through the downpour, leaving the irate woman behind, shouting abuse at Denise's tail.

~ ~ ~

Drenched and carrying her discarded shoes, Denise rushed entered the office, locking the door behind her. Holding her chest to prevent her thumping heart from escaping it, she took a moment leaning against to the door, to calm down. A melancholy glance at the family photo on the wall was enough to motivate her. Anticipating unwelcome visitors, she hurried to her desk, powered up her Mac, inserted a floppy disk, opened a file, and began typing feverishly.

~ ~ ~

When I read the footnote, tears welled up in my eyes. In the first-person narrative, it read, "It is only a matter of time before I receive a visit from my tail. All in all for the disk… but the note from Eisha will stay behind the family..." The message was cryptic.

"Is that all she wrote?" I asked.

"Yep, she never finished it."

"It pretty much confirms she was murdered by the tail, doesn't it?" I said, my voice catching in my throat. Childhood memories of my beloved mother flashed before my mind's eye.

"She said, 'all in all for the disk,' that's a reference to Another Brick in the Wall where we found the disk, but what did she mean by 'the note from Eisha will stay behind the family...?'"

I took a deep breath, shifting from grief to determination. I got up and paced the office, thinking out loud, "Another cryptic message. So, let's assume she finishes writing…" I envisioned my mother sitting in the same room, at the desk in front of her Mac. "So, she's sitting where you are now… she ejects the disk, gets up, goes to the wall, removes the Pink Floyd photo, takes out the brick, then stashes the disk. She replaces the brick…"

"Why doesn't she hide the note there as well?"

"Ah, now that's an old Danny Davis trick."

"Who's Danny Davis?"

"A Carter Stone PI in the books. Danny would never keep more than one secret thing in the same place. So, 'stay behind the family' is the key."

I followed the ethereal vision of my mother into the main office. It wasn't eerie; it felt as though it was meant to be. Intrigued by my actions, Kendy followed. I watched my mother go barefoot to the family photo. There was a sudden rattle at the door, which caught her attention. She stared sharply at a shadow on the other side of the frosted door glass, and then it shattered… and my vision vanished. I approached the family photo on the wall, removed it, and checked the back. "Behind the family," I muttered. When I removed the backplate in the frame, I found the note.

"Brilliant!" Kendy exclaimed.

I didn't mention to Kendy that my discovery had been inspired by seeing the apparition of my mother. I placed the frame on the couch, unfurled the note, and read it aloud, "It says PAN AM Flight 103, December 18, 1988."

CHAPTER
FIFTEEN

I was pacing the floor while Kendy was on the laptop Googling the find.

"Check this out. Dec 18, 1988 - PAN AM Flight 103 Explodes Over Lockerbie, Scotland."

I looked at the photographic montage on the screen, then flopped into the chair, stunned. "This has all been about the terrorist attack that downed a PAN AM 747 in 1988. My folks were killed because of it."

Kendy read out more details, "Two hundred and forty-three passengers, 16 crew, and 11 residents of Lockerbie, Scotland, killed. Libyans were blamed... Get this... Bengt Nilsson UN Assistant Secretary-General and UN Commissioner for Namibia was Lockerbie's highest-profile victim."

"There you go," it was a lightbulb moment, "he nominated Daniel Anderson for the Golden Dawn. So wait a minute, Ann Temple said Anderson murdered the government official from Namibia... there's a major connection here. Why was Nilsson on that flight?"

Kendy went surfing again and came up with something, "He took Flight 103 en-route to UN HQ in New York to present evidence of corruption by Iran, South Africa, and Britain in the Rossing Uranium mine dispute."

"Aha, so, what if Anderson was a double agent for NIS and CIA, and was undercover to befriend Nilsson? He learns the flight is going to be sabotaged, comes to New York to blow the whistle, but before he can, he gets chopped into pieces?"

Kendy swivelled around from the laptop. "I don't get it, like who blew up the plane? Libyans were blamed."

I was up pacing the floor again. "What if they were set up by the partners in the Uranium mine... that would explain why Farzin Rashidi was so desperate to shut down publication of the book? Ann Temple said he was on the board of the Rossing mine for Iran."

"Eisha was Libyan; she must've overheard Ajeeb arranging the bombing. I wonder if Dumbo Removals like still exists?" She swivelled back and searched. "No... but get this, in 1990: The Bashir family, owners of Dumbo Removal Company NYC, were deported to Libya in connection to the downing of PAN AM Flight 103."

"I'm not surprised after the shootout with Denise, Blake, and the agents. Did she ever ascertain whether they were CIA or FBI?"

"No, why?"

"You better go home now, Kendy; I'll drop you off on the way to pick up Santana from the airport."

~ ~ ~

Kendy looked around the interior of my Tesla as if it were a Rolls-Royce. "Wow, nice car. I didn't know you owned a Tesla. It's so quiet; you can't even hear the engine running."

I drove out of the Regis basement car park into James Street traffic.

"It's brand new, but I never use it. I bought it to sit in and think."

"Think?"

"Yeah, the smell of new leather upholstery gets me into a flow state."

"Well, you better do some flow state thinking on the way to JFK because you've got to like decode those numbers."

"2237864538, I'm processing them."

I parked outside Kendy's apartment block. She got out and looked back in, "Catch you in the morning, boss."

"Bell me if you need to. I figure it's going to be an all-nighter for me."

She closed the door, and I pulled out into the traffic with the number 2237864538 circulating in my brain like the hook of a great song. I headed for the Williamsburg Bridge on the 278, so I could link with the Van Wyck Expressway. I cranked up my Pink Floyd compilation; the first track up was 'Echoes,' and it certainly slipped me into an alpha state to think. In no time flat, I found myself entering the airport heading for Terminal 8. I pulled up outside the American Airlines terminal to wait for Carlos. I just happened to look up into the rear-view mirror in time to catch a female parking cop materialise out of the darkness; she was making a beeline for me. "She must have been bloody lurking behind a pole or something?" I grumbled as I lowered the window.

She looked in. "You'll need to move the vehicle now, sir, or I'll issue you a citation."

I turned down the music, attempting to buy time for Santana to arrive, and decided to use my charm. "Sorry, officer, I didn't hear you. What was that?"

She rolled her eyes, clearly annoyed, and was just about to write a ticket when a hand reached from behind her, holding an LAPD badge.

"Detective Inspector Santana LAPD," a familiar voice announced, "this is my ride, officer."

She stepped out of the way to reveal Carlos; he got into the car.

"Good to see you, Carlos. Lucky you recognised my car."

"What with a plate that says Axis? Get out of here," he chuckled in his characteristic style as we shook hands. "Nice wheels. Okay, you've got between here and Manhattan to fill me in."

~ ~ ~

Carlos was on the couch, and I grabbed two glasses and a bottle of rye. I took the armchair opposite him, poured a couple of fingers in each glass, and we toasted.

"Good times," Carlos said. "So, you think Bolt is connected to whoever is still trying, after over 30 years, to cover up one, the real ID of the severed arm, and two the plot that downed PAN AM Flight 103?"

"Bottom line in answer to both questions is it will show up who murdered my folks."

"And Liz Parks… It stinks of a Firm conspiracy, son."

"I hear you."

"You know the drill; we'll need to flush Bolt out."

I topped up the drinks. Carlos pulled an iPad out of his kitbag.

"First we need to solve the paradox left by the old man, 2237864538."

Carlos loosened his bolo slide ready for work, opened his iPad, and continued, "There's probably enough in that bottle to solve it. Let's get on with it."

~ ~ ~

Kendy glanced up from her desk at us entering the office.

"Kendy, come out here."

She joined us. "Ah, this must be the infamous Carlos Santana."

"Got it in one, Kendy," Carlos said with a big smile.

"You guys look a bit under the weather; grab some coffee, it's done."

I got two mugs and poured us a brew. Handed Carlos his. We all took seats, and I told Kendy, "Cracked the code."

Carlos winked at Kendy, "Took till dawn and a bottle of rye."

Kendy was on the edge of the couch, eager to hear. "Well, like how?"

I got up, went to Kendy's room, and wheeled in a whiteboard. On it, I wrote the name Carter Stone and underneath each letter, I assigned a number. Carter was 123453, and then Stone was 64785. Then I wrote the number my father had written on the paper: 2237864538.

"So, if we extrapolate this note number by using the

corresponding numbers from the name Carter Stone, we get..." I drew lines from the letters corresponding to the numbers. "Aaron Stern... the name of the man belonging to the severed arm."

Kendy was on her feet, "Far out! Like how brilliant... how did your dad have time to come up with that?"

"I'm amazed my mother didn't get it. Dad often used names in code in his books."

"So Daniel Anderson's alias was like Aaron Stern," Kendy confirmed.

Carlos was smiling, "Yep. So, now I need to access FBI and CIA databases for that name, but I left my damn iPad at the apartment."

While I parked the whiteboard, Kendy fetched her laptop from her office and gave it to Carlos.

"His security clearance will give him special access to those databases," I explained.

"Well, up to a certain level. What do you know, an immediate hit." He looked at me wide-eyed. "Aaron Stern was an FBI operative, MIA, 1988."

"MIA?" Kendy repeated.

"Missing in action," I explained.

The door buzzer sounded. Kendy jumped up and checked the video. "It's Bulldog." She buzzed him in.

"I don't get it..." Kendy said with a puzzled look.

Bulldog came to the door, and she let him in. I made the introduction. "Detective Santana, Detective Bixby."

"Call me Carlos."

"Call me Bulldog," he said, shaking Carlos' hand. "Incredible what you told me on the phone. I'm late because I accessed the NYPD database on Aaron Stern; it linked with the FBI. Stern, MIA, was Rixon's operative. Then, I found a bizarre connection, two years ago Rixon was on a case in Vegas involving someone Carlos had mentioned, a guy named Al Head."

Carlos was nodding, "There you go, the link we were after. I think the time has come to set up a meeting with Agent Rixon."

I grabbed my phone and called him. "Rixon… Axis Stone. I've got news… I've broken the case. Where? The Hyphen, 61, done. You'll text it… okay." I terminated the call. The eyes of Santana, Bulldog, and Kendy were on me. "It's on," I said. "The Hyphen in an hour. He'll be there alone doing a terrorism risk assessment of Track 61. I'm to go alone."

This time Santana was vigorously shaking his head, "No way, I didn't come all this way to attend your funeral, son."

"I'd put my money on this guy Rixon killing Stern, Liz Parks, and goodness knows who else. He's a rogue agent," Bulldog growled.

"He must've been ordered to keep the planned bombing of Flight 103 a secret, that's why he killed Aaron Stern."

"I'd say he was on the Iran payroll to set Libya up as scapegoats. I'm going in alone; I need proof he took out my folks. If I'm not out in twenty minutes, send in the cavalry," I said emphatically, eyeballing Carlos. "I need to do this, mate."

"Alright, alright, I know you do, I get it… Heard it before, haven't I? What the hell is this Track 61 anyway, Bulldog?"

~ ~ ~

I drove into the underground car park of the Waldorf Astoria.

Bulldog had explained, "Track 61 is an abandoned platform of the Metro-North, Manhattan subway beneath the Waldorf-Astoria Hotel. The hotel's nickname is the Hyphen."

Carlos had reacted in a manner to be expected. "You need your head read going down into the bowels of New York with Rixon, son." Always looking after my butt, like the father I never had.

~ ~ ~

I parked the Tesla, got out, and began walking in the dim light, each step resonating in the vast concrete grotto. I stopped and checked the text of directions from Rixon. It said to proceed to a door marked: Authorized Entry Only. I saw it up ahead, went to it, and opened it. Beyond it was a room with a big sliding door for an oversized elevator. I pressed the call button. It all looked well past its use-by-date. A loud servo sounded… it felt like it was taking ages, finally it arrived, and the door lazily slid open. Rixon was standing on the other side.

"Come in," he said. I thought, 'said the spider to the fly.' The interior was large enough to take a car. We stood apart, wary of one another. Rixon pressed the single 'down' button on the old control panel… the elevator jerked and then started a creaky descent.

"President Franklin D. Roosevelt didn't want the public to see he was a paraplegic, so he used this elevator to take his car down to his personal train carriage on Track 61. Quite a history Track 61."

"I didn't come for a history lesson," I snarled. The elevator came to an abrupt stop—the door opened, and Rixon led me out. A few lights revealed the lost world of the long-disused subway in situ. A dusty, rusty, relic of a bygone era. In the ghostly shadows, a train carriage and sections of track dissolved into the pitch darkness.

Rixon stopped. We faced off. A servo sounded as the elevator returned to basement level.

"Okay, what have you got?"

"Aaron Stern and Pan Am Flight 103," I said firmly.

"There's always collateral damage in international affairs, Stone; we deal with circumstances, and sacrifices are made by few for the benefit of many. Stern and your folks were some of those sacrifices."

"Along with 270 people with Flight 103, Liz Parks, and how many others?"

"Thousands, all to keep the peace and freedom for the generations since to enjoy."

"You make it sound so patriotic, but I have a different take… you see, I think you're a double agent. When your operative Aaron Stern told you the secret plan he'd uncovered, you decided to sell it to Rashidi and in league with him, you set up the Libyans through Ajeeb Bashir to take the fall for the downing of Pan Am 103."

"That's about as fanciful as one of your father's fiction fantasies."

"He didn't write fantasy... you set me up to chase my dad's kidnappers as a ruse. You thought you'd killed two birds with one stone, getting rid of Bengt Nilsson from blowing the whistle on the illegal uranium mine in Namibia for Iran, and getting Libya blamed so Gaddafi could be stopped from unifying Africa."

"Gaddafi and his thugs needed to be stopped."

"That might be, but it's cretins like you, Rixon, that embody everything rotten about mankind. You murdered my folks," I growled.

"Damn right I took them out, they'd been warned. It's time!" he called out loud.

Handerson Bolt stepped out of the darkness with a gun aimed at me.

I shouted, "Ah, yes, your Al Head mafia connection Handerson Bolt. Cheap murdering mercenary... I rest my case." I caught movement off to my left... another guy brandishing a gun had slid out from hiding. "And I bet you're missing a pinky," I said to him.

"Goodbye, Stone," Rixon snarled and then turned his back on me and walked away. I watched him walk to the elevator and press the call button.

"Get on your knees, Stone, with your hands behind your head," Bolt snarled. "Now! Pinky."

I didn't have any choice but to comply. Pinky moved quickly and pushed a gun against the back of my head.

"Two in the back of the head... isn't that your signature, Bolt?"

"Farewell, Stone," Bolt sneered.

A shot resounded, I flinched, and Pinky's head exploded.

I quickly executed a forward paratrooper's roll, drew my gun from the back of my pants in the move, propped myself up on one elbow, took aim, and put two slugs in rapid succession into Bolt's chest. It was excellent grouping. The big man's legs crumbled; and he peeled off a shot on the way down that just missed me.

Santana stepped out of the darkness with a smoking gun.

Getting up, I greeted him, "Glad you made it, buddy."

Rixon had turned away from the elevator door, drawn his gun, and has it aimed at me.

"Nice try, Stone," Rixon bellowed as the elevator doors opened behind him.

"Drop it, Rixon!" Bulldog's gruff voice commanded. He and four cops emerged from the elevator, forced Rixon to his knees, and then cuffed him.

~ ~ ~

I was sitting in bed with lovely Lisa, her librarian look cast aside, both of us covered only by the bedsheet from the waist down.

"Wow. That's quite a story. So, how did Santana make his way down to Track 61?"

"There's another secret entrance on East 50th Street, just to the left of the Waldorf Towers. He did an impressive job finding his way to me all alone through the inky darkness."

"Terrifying. So, what's next for the manuscript?"

"Maybe I'll complete it and seek publication."

"Didn't your parents sign a contract not to publish it?"

"They sure did... but I didn't." I gave her pink nipple a playful tweak.

She smiled seductively, "Is that meant to arouse me again?"

"Absolutely."

"Well, it certainly did the job."

"I always get the job done, baby." I reached for the bedside lamp and switched it off.

"Ummm, you certainly do, Axis Stone."

The End

Don't miss the next thrilling adventure
in book five:

GOD'S DOOR